GUBLAK'S GREED

This is Angus's Book

By the same author

HAGBANE'S DOOM
THE HEALTHY ALTERNATIVE

GUBLAK'S GREED

John Houghton

KINGSWAY PUBLICATIONS
EASTBOURNE

ISBN 0 86065 366 8

Front cover design by Vic Mitchell

Printed in Great Britain for
KINGSWAY PUBLICATIONS LTD
Lottbridge Drove, Eastbourne, E. Sussex BN23 6NT by
Cox & Wyman Ltd, Reading.
Typeset by Central Southern Typesetters, Eastbourne,
E. Sussex.

Contents

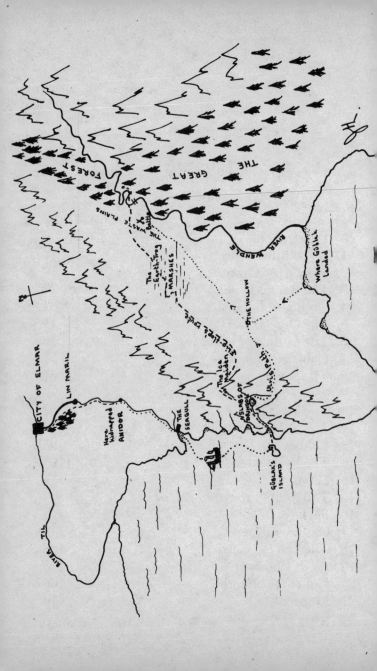

To our friend
Christine Smith

Prologue

Gold glittered in the flickering candlelight. A fat green goblin sat cross-legged in the midst of his treasure. He ran his spiny fingers through a pile of jewels. His name was Gublak and his eyes were greedy with desire.

'Pretty things,' he breathed. 'So shiny and so precious. But I want something more; more than this can give me.' He licked his lips hungrily as he drooled over his hoard.

A knock on the door followed by a call from one of his servants disturbed his thoughts.

'Beg pardon, your Eminence, but the visitor has arrived.'

The goblin grunted and reluctantly left his treasure in order to meet his guest.

They spoke in the topmost room of Gublak's island fortress. Only the moon gave any light and thick shadows hung in black drapes about the cold stone walls. The air was still.

'I believe the time is near and soon you shall have what you desire,' said the visitor.

Gublak's eyes gleamed in the moonlight. 'Good. If what you say is true, your reward shall be great. Tell me what you know.'

The mysterious visitor unfolded his dark scheme. 'It will not be difficult to take her captive,' he concluded.

'Excellent, excellent!' The goblin paced the room, rubbing his hands together. 'And then it will be mine. How I have desired that jewel! Many months have I waited for such a moment. You bring good news tonight and I am well pleased.' He turned sharply on his guest. 'But do not fail me now, I warn you. I must possess that magic stone. Failure means death for you, do you understand?'

'I shall not fail you,' the visitor answered evenly. 'If all the preparations are made according to plan, nothing can go wrong.'

Gublak nodded curtly. The interview was over and the visitor departed soundlessly. Far below, the howl of a wolf chilled the night air.

.   .   *   .   .

Oswain stirred fitfully in his sleep. Something was tugging at his mind. He began to dream.

A glistening pearl floated upon a dark green sea over which a storm was brewing. It broke suddenly and with such violence that the fragile gem seemed certain to be shattered by the fury of the waves. But just as all appeared lost, the peak of an ice-capped mountain arose from the raging sea and carried the pearl to safety. Higher and higher it climbed until the sea was no more to be seen and all was still. At once, the jewel burst into brilliant light and shone like a star from the mountain-top.

Oswain awoke with a start.

Not long after, in the cold hour before dawn, he stood by Elmere, the Star-Pool, in the enchanted glade of the Great Forest. The fragrance of the air and the life which flowed from the Merestone* cleared his head and cheered his heart. Yet the unease which had broken his sleep remained with him.

'Elmesh guide me,' he whispered as he gazed into the gently glowing pool. For a moment he saw only his own reflection. Then the waters swirled and he beheld the face of a young princess. She seemed in much distress and the howling of wolves filled Oswain's mind.

'Alena!' he breathed.

---

*You can read about this in *Hagbane's Doom*.

Chapter One

ALENA RUNS AWAY

'I'm fed up with everything!'

Princess Alena's private bedroom overlooked the splendid palace gardens. Beyond lay the fine white buildings of the City of Elmar, capital of the West and home to the royal family. The summer air was warm, the scent of honeysuckle sweet and the flowerbeds a celebration of colour; but this did nothing to lessen the princess's foul mood.

She sat on the broad sill of the latticed window, kicking her heels against the wall.

'I mean, look at it all,' she continued. 'Same old room, same old days. Get up, get dressed, be on my best behaviour. Meet the guests. Smile at everyone. I'm sick and tired of smiling! Why can't I do something different?'

The princess was not talking to herself. Perched on the back of a chair was a large black crow who listened, bright eyed, to everything she said.

She dropped down from the window sill and wandered over to the wardrobe mirror where she scowled at her reflection. The princess had beautiful golden tresses but today she yanked them impatiently.

'Look at my hair. Why can't I have it short like

everyone else? I hate brushing it every day. Same with all these clothes.' She eyed the blue brocade gown she wore. 'I just want to wear ordinary things sometimes.'

'It sounds as if you don't want to be a princess any more,' the black crow cawed.

She flopped on her bed and heaved a great sigh. 'No, it's not that really, I suppose. It's just, well . . . I want some adventure, that's all. It's so boring being a princess all the time. I'd like to do something different. You understand, don't you, Crow?'

Crow nodded. 'Then why don't you? I mean, if you *want* adventure, you can have it. What's to stop you?'

'My parents,' she shot back. 'They won't let me. All they say is, I must behave like a princess—and I'll be happy when I do. Huh!'

She lay silent for a few moments, then abruptly rolled on to her front and cupped her head in her hands. She smiled at Crow.

'I tell you what. Why don't we run away from home for a while?'

Crow gazed at her intently but said nothing.

'You'd come with me, wouldn't you, Crow? Oh, please say you'll come with me. We could have wonderful adventures together, and do all the things you've been telling me about. It'll be so much better than here.

'We'll have to go secretly, of course,' she continued excitedly. 'It's the only way. But it will make it even more fun.'

'How will you avoid being recognized?' Crow asked.

'That's no problem. I'll disguise myself as an ordinary girl.'

13

She rolled off the bed and returned to the mirror. 'I'm sure we can find some old clothes in the servants' quarters. And I'll cut my hair,' she cried enthusiastically. 'Then nobody will recognize me. What do you think, Crow?'

The bird nodded his head in approval.

'Then you agree? Oh, it'll be marvellous.' She turned eagerly towards him. 'Come on, where shall we go? What shall we do? Will it be far? I don't want to go *too* far.'

Crow suggested they aim for the seaside, which she thought was a marvellous idea. So, for the rest of that afternoon they plotted and planned their great adventure, and it was not until late in the evening that Crow eventually flew noiselessly away into the gathering dusk.

Princess Alena undressed slowly. As she did so, she toyed with the pearl which hung from a slender silver chain about her neck. This was none other than the famed Star-Pearl of Elmar, so named because of the blue star which burned within its depths. The princess had worn it for as long as she could remember.

It was her birth stone—her name meant Starborn—and it made her think of her parents. For a moment she hesitated in her resolve to run away. It seemed as if the pearl was gently tugging at her mind. But then a determined look came into her eyes.

'No, I will do it. I've always wanted to and now I've made up my mind,' she declared out loud. 'And I don't care.'

And with that she prepared for bed.

.   .   *   .   .

Two days later Princess Alena celebrated the arrival of her fifteenth birthday by cutting off all her golden tresses.

Then she donned the peasant's outfit which she had secured from one of the serving maids on the pretence that it was for a dressing-up game. She took a last satisfied glance in the mirror and announced to Crow that she was ready. It was five o'clock in the morning.

Quietly, she opened the latticed window and let down the knotted sheets which she had already tied to the bedpost.

'Make sure the coast is clear, Crow. I don't want to get caught half way down the wall.'

Crow assured her that all was quiet, so she swung a bag across her shoulder, slipped over the side and slid to the ground. The effort left her puffing and blowing, so they paused a moment until she got her breath back.

Keeping close to the house and ducking below the ground-floor windows she crept to a long low hedge which ran to the far garden wall. With a quick glance to the left and right, she darted behind it and crouched her way along its length. An old tree which grew by the wall and whose branches overhung the street provided the way out. Swiftly scaling it, she crossed the wall and took from her bag a short length of rope which she had brought for this moment. She tied it to one of the boughs and slithered down to the roadway. In a matter of minutes she was clear of the palace. She blew on her chafed hands but otherwise looked very pleased with herself. Nobody had spotted her so far.

'Well done, mistress,' whispered Crow. 'That's the most difficult bit over and done with.'

She gave him a cheerful grin.

The streets of the city were quiet at this early hour, with only the occasional noise to force the two runaways into nervous hiding. As often as not it proved to be no more than a cat searching for breakfast down an alley.

It took them nearly half an hour of weaving in and out of the side streets to reach the city gates. They arrived just as the watchmen were opening them for the farm labourers to depart for their day's work in the fields.

'This is your chance,' urged Crow. 'Get in among them so you won't be noticed.'

Princess Alena seized her opportunity, and shuffled unnoticed amidst the small crowd of workers and animals which bustled through the gates. Before very long they were alone on the open road.

'Phew, we've done it!' cried the Princess. 'I'm free at last. No more rules and regulations. No more good manners. And no more lessons. I can do what I like from now on. This is what I call a *real* birthday.'

Crow nodded enthusiastically. 'Yes, but we mustn't dilly-dally just yet, mistress. It can't be too long before they discover you are missing and start searching for you.'

'You're right, Crow,' said the princess matter-of-factly. 'But first we must hide this.' She opened her shoulder bag, revealing her shorn locks.

'I had to bring it all with me,' she explained. 'Otherwise somebody might find it and realize I've changed how I look. But we must get rid of it now. Any ideas?'

Crow found a ditch behind a hedgerow and she threw the hair into that. Then she covered it with stones and torn grass. Satisfied with her handiwork, she was ready for the journey.

Although there was a road which ran from Elmar

to Lin Maril, it was too well used for their purposes. However, a hundred metres or so off the road lay a long stretch of woodland, and they chose this as the most secluded route.

It was another one of those warm summer days and the princess felt she hadn't a care in the world. The rich earthy smell of the woods delighted her as she picked wild flowers and chased squirrels to her heart's content.

'I've not felt so happy in years, Crow. This really is the best idea ever.'

The morning passed quickly and, in spite of the princess's diversions, they made good progress. When lunchtime came she sprawled beneath the shade of an old oak tree while Crow perched on a low branch above her, keeping a sharp lookout. She ate from the bag of food which she had brought, then snoozed contentedly for an hour or so in the hot sun.

It was Crow's gentle nudging which aroused her. 'We must be on our way,' he cawed as she stirred.

'Oh, Crow, why?' she murmured sleepily. 'There's no hurry, is there? And I was enjoying my nap, too.'

'No, I suppose not,' he replied. 'But if you want to get to the seaside we'll have to keep moving. I reckon it's all of four days from the city.'

'All right then.' She smiled as she struggled to her feet. 'I'm coming. Oo! Ouch! I do feel stiff.'

They travelled uneventfully until early evening when they reached the outskirts of Lin Maril, a small but busy town. The woodland changed to fields so they rejoined the road but had scarcely been on it for more than a few minutes when a clatter of hooves behind them caused the princess to dart for cover behind a tree. A company of soldiers on horseback, royal guards, flashed by in a cloud of dust.

'They're out looking for me,' she muttered. 'You'd better go spy out the land, Crow.'

The bird flew into the town where, perching unnoticed by an open window, he overheard a soldier's conversation with the mayor. The princess's parents, he learned, had discovered her departure when they entered her room laden with birthday presents at eight o'clock that morning. The alarm was raised and soldiers had been out searching ever since. The aging king was beside himself with anxiety and the queen had been in tears for most of the day. Their first thought was that she had been kidnapped, and every house in the city had been searched, for nobody had departed the gates under suspicious circumstances. However, during the afternoon a sharp-eyed workman had made the awful discovery of the princess's hair in a ditch and the search had been flung far and wide since then.

The soldiers' news put the whole town on the alert, so the princess obviously could not spend the night there. Crow swiftly returned and reported his findings to her. But he didn't tell her how upset her parents were.

'Well, I can't stay in Lin Maril, that's for sure,' she said. 'No matter. I'll do what I've always wanted to do. I'm going to sleep under the stars!'

They found a sheltered grassy bank beside a small stream where the princess lay down under the comforting gaze of the moon and, wearied by her journey, soon fell fast asleep. Crow kept an unblinking watch over her.

Chapter Two

THE GYPSY CARAVAN

The following morning Princess Alena awoke early, much refreshed. The sun was up and she danced merrily in the brook, splashing and laughing to her heart's content.

'Not so loud, mistress,' Crow cautioned anxiously.

'Oh, don't worry. Nobody's awake yet except me, and I'm so happy,' she cried.

Just then she trod on a very sharp stone.

'Ouch! That hurt!'

She hobbled from the stream to find she had cut the ball of her foot.

'Serves me right, I suppose,' she grimaced. 'Still, it doesn't look bad, and we're going to have another super day, aren't we, Crow?'

Crow seemed worried, but she put her sandal on and assured him she could walk without difficulty.

Breakfast exhausted the food supplies she had brought, but that didn't dampen her spirits in the least.

'We'll live off the land, won't we? I mean, that's what you do, isn't it, Crow? Though I'm not eating the things you like. Ugh!' She made a gesture of disgust as she thought of dining on slugs and worms. 'No, I mean, I'll eat fruit and berries. You can tell me which ones are safe. Look, those are blackberries over there, aren't they?'

She hobbled across and tried some. 'Mm, delicious. We'll find lots more on the way, I'm sure.'

It took them about an hour of criss-crossing footpaths to skirt Lin Maril and find their way back on to the little-used road to Anidor. All the while they had to keep themselves hidden from suspicious eyes and many times Crow flew around to make sure the coast was clear. Neither relished the thought of being discovered.

There was one tense moment when a farm dog caught wind of the princess and began to bark loudly. The only thing Crow could do was to cause a commotion among the hens until the farmer chased him off, assuming this to be the reason for his dog barking. Nothing else hindered them from their journey.

As the morning wore on, Princess Alena's feet began to ache, especially the wounded one, and by lunchtime she was limping quite badly. She was also becoming hungry.

'Whew! I'll have to rest a while, Crow,' she called to the hovering bird and plonked herself on the grassy verge. 'My foot hurts so much. Can you see any food around?'

'Not here,' was the reply.

'Oh, never mind. We'll come across some soon, I expect.'

She struggled to her feet and staggered on. But after another half-mile she had had enough. Her spirits were dropping and hunger and thirst were finally taking the glamour off the whole ill-considered adventure.

'Can't you find food anywhere, Crow?' she cried impatiently.

The bird flew off in a wide circle. He was soon back.

'Good news,' he cawed. 'There's a bit of woodland not far away, with water and plenty of berries.'

'Then take me to it!' she replied with revived enthusiasm.

Sure enough, he led her to a beautiful copse teeming with blackberries. The princess ate greedily, but was still hungry—and her foot was by now badly swollen.

It was just then that she spied a gypsy caravan stationed in a clearing. A man and a woman were cooking their dinner over an open fire. The breeze wafted a delicious aroma of stew towards her, which set her mouth watering. She edged closer.

'Do you think they would know who I am, Crow?' she whispered.

He hesitated for a moment.

'No, I'm sure they wouldn't recognize you,' he replied. 'Anyway, the gypsies prefer to have as little to do with the soldiers as they can. News won't have reached them yet.'

'Well, what do you think? Shall I ask them for food—and something for my foot?'

'I think you should,' he encouraged.

So the princess hobbled painfully across to the couple, who looked up as a twig cracked beneath her feet.

'Why, hallo, missy,' the man called out after a friendly fashion. 'This is a surprise. We don't see many folks in these parts. Come and join us. We're just about to have lunch.'

The princess was greatly relieved that they seemed friendly, and delighted at the mention of lunch.

The woman smiled at her. 'You look hungry, m'dear. Come and sit y'self down now. We got rabbit stew and plenty of bread, so help yourself.'

'Oo, thank you,' she replied. 'I really am hungry. It's very kind of you.'

'Think nothing of it,' the woman answered. 'We always offer what hospitality we have to folks that passes through.'

The princess tucked into the meal with relish and the gypsies watched her in half-amusement.

'You were hungry, weren't you?' said the man. 'Must've been a fair distance y've come.'

'Mmm, all the way from Elmar since yesterday. I . . . I'm on my way to see my uncle at the seaside,' she lied.

That was the first of many untruths she had to tell in answer to their questions over the meal, for Princess Alena discovered that a lie once sown soon produces a harvest of more lies. Feeling bad about it, she made to get up as soon as the meal was over, but her foot caused her to wince.

'Why, you've hurt your foot, m'dear,' said the woman. 'Come into the caravan a moment and I'll see what I can do for it.'

'Oo, I've never been inside a real gypsy caravan before,' replied the princess. 'And my foot does hurt. If you don't mind . . . .'

'Of course not. It'll be my pleasure.'

The woman led the way while her husband helped the princess up the steps and through the door. The inside was gloomy and smelt musty. She strained her eyes to see.

'Over here, m'dear,' said the woman.

She stumbled against something and, all at once, a small globe began to glow with an unnatural pale light. The princess gave a start.

'W. . .w. . .what's that?' she stammered.

'Why you're in luck, child,' exclaimed the gypsy

woman. 'My crystal ball has something to show you. Take a closer look. Don't be afraid now.'

The princess hesitated. She had been taught from an early age to avoid strange people with magic charms and crystal balls.

'Go on,' urged the woman from behind her. 'It won't hurt you.'

Still she held back.

Exotic shapes passed across the globe. Its light was hypnotic, strangely attractive. Curiosity tugged at the princess and, in a moment of pride, believing she could handle matters, she cast aside her doubts and peered into the ball.

A whirring sound filled her ears and her eyes began to sting. She felt giddy and sick. Summoning all her strength she sought to turn away, but could not. Then something entered her mind like the stab of a knife. She gave a cry and collapsed into unconsciousness.

A pair of strong hands grasped her limp body and lowered her on to a couch. Two pairs of eyes glowed with evil satisfaction in the gloom.

Crow was winging his way south-east towards the sea.

.　　.　　*　　.　　.

Princess Alena's head felt fit to burst. She winced at the never-ending clatter of saucepans and crockery which accompanied the caravan's jolting, jangling journey along the bumpy roads.

Time passed like a bad dream in the gloom of her mobile prison; she had no idea how long she had lain unconscious or whether it was night or day. All she knew was that her head hurt and she was desperately thirsty—and she could not move.

In fact, some twenty-four hours had passed since her capture, and during that time her kidnappers had covered much ground, mostly by means of little-known byways. Their direction lay always towards the sea.

The princess tested her bonds once more, but to no avail. Her wrists and ankles were firmly tied together by loops of rope running beneath the couch. There seemed no way of escape.

Her thoughts turned again to what had happened. What a fool she had been! The course of events raced through her mind up to the moment when she had looked into the crystal ball. Then pain gripped her head afresh and her brain seemed filled with frightening jabbering voices. She wondered what had happened to Crow. He was her only hope. Perhaps he was following the caravan. Or maybe he had gone to fetch help from the soldiers.

Her train of thought broke as the caravan rattled to a standstill. She waited with bated breath. At length, the door opened and she screwed her eyes at the sudden light. The gypsy man entered carrying a dish and a mug. She drew back apprehensively.

'Food for you, missy.' He spoke softly but there was no kindness in his eyes.

He loosed her hands and she sat up stiffly, rubbing her wrists.

'No funny business now or else . . .' he threatened and offered her the mug of water. She drank eagerly and felt instantly better.

'Why have you done this to me?' she demanded, more bravely than she felt. 'You've no right to take me prisoner like this. Let me go at once or else you'll be in real trouble.'

The gypsy laughed. 'Cocky little thing, aren't you?'

24

But it won't do you no good. Now, come on, eat this grub 'cos I haven't got all day to waste.'

'Don't want it,' she pouted.

'I said, eat it,' retorted the man angrily.

'Shan't.'

The gypsy drew back his hand and made to strike her. Sullenly, she took the plate and ate the food. He watched her carefully.

'That's better. Do as you're told and no harm'll come to you. Now lie down again.'

The princess, knowing she could do nothing, obeyed and lay sobbing as her wrists were retied and the man withdrew from the caravan. Minutes later they were on the move again.

The journey seemed to last for ever. Occasionally they stopped and she was fed by the man or his woman. Sometimes she slept for a while, but bad dreams kept waking her. At last they seemed to reach their destination, for the caravan stopped a long while. She could hear the squealing of seagulls.

'Oh, if only I hadn't run away,' she thought miserably. 'I'd have never landed in this mess. What do they want with me? What's going to happen?'

As if in answer to her questions, the door opened with a bang and the gypsy strode in. He released her bonds but held her tightly by the arm as he dragged her up from the couch.

'Come on,' he growled and thrust her towards the door. 'This is where you get off.'

She stumbled down the steps. Everything was shrouded in mist, except for a vicious-looking sailor who stood before them. She looked in vain for Crow.

'Here she is, then,' said the gypsy.

'And not before time either,' the other answered. 'The cap'n don't like to be kept waiting, y'know.'

The gypsy spat on the ground. 'I can't help that.

25

We got 'er 'ere as fast as we could. Give us the gold and we'll be on our way.'

The sailor scowled and threw a small leather bag to the gypsy who caught it deftly and thrust the princess forward at the same time. She stumbled, then caught her balance and made to flee, but the sailor was too quick for her. He grabbed her wrist and pulled her towards him. She struggled and bit his finger hard, an action which, though it earned her a hard cuff round the ear, gave her some small comfort. With a curse the sailor dragged her off to a small shack and threw her inside. Bolting the door after him he left the princess alone, crying on the floor.

Chapter Three

THE ROUND HOLE

'It's very deep,' declared Sarah.

'Yes, and no fence around it either,' said her elder brother Peter. 'I wouldn't like to be walking across here in the dark.'

'Just imagine, though,' Andrew enthused, 'you could be running across the grass chased by a ferocious tiger and suddenly you see this in front of you and you swerve out of the way at the last minute and the tiger goes "Aaagh!" and crashes to its doom.'

'There aren't any tigers in England,' retorted his brother.

'What about in safari parks?'

'But not here in Cornwall.'

'I bet there are.'

'Oh, shush, you two!'

The three Brown children were on holiday at a place called Trevone, and they were staring down a huge round hole sunk into the low northern cliff of the sandy inlet—about twenty-five metres from its edge. The hole was some thirty-five metres across and as many deep. At the bottom ran an arched tunnel of dripping rock which led to the sea. They planned to climb down this hole and work their way through the slippery tunnel and out on to the rocky

27

coastline.

Peter went first and slithered rapidly to the bottom. Sarah followed more cautiously.

'Hurry up,' urged Andrew from behind her.

'I'm doing my best,' she gasped. 'Don't rush me or I'll fall.'

'You're doing fine,' Peter shouted. 'Come on, it's all right.'

A couple of minutes later Sarah and Andrew slid down the last few metres and joined him.

'Phew, it doesn't half make you grubby,' said Andrew, studying his dirty hands and the seat of his shorts.

'Just mind you don't wipe them on your tee-shirt or you'll be in trouble from Mum,' his sister retorted. 'She doesn't want to be washing on holiday.'

'Look, there's the tunnel,' said Peter. He indicated the split rock to their right.

'Come on then. Let's go!' cried Andrew.

They made their way along the broad passage, shouting as they went to make their voices boom off the damp walls. It brought them out on to a wild coast of broken rocks between which ran the sea. behind stood the sheer cliff face.

'Cor, let's go rock hopping,' said Andrew. 'The tide's still low, so we've plenty of time.'

The others agreed and for the next quarter of an hour they enjoyed themselves clambering over the barnacled rocks. So much so that not one of them noticed the strange mist rapidly creeping across the sea towards them. At least, not until Peter suddenly realized he couldn't see Sarah, and it was cold.

'Hey, what's happened? Andrew, Sarah, where are you?'

'Over here.' Their voices sounded muffled in the mist.

It took a couple of minutes to find one another, by which time the mist was so thick that the cliff was only a dim shadow behind them.

'We'd better get back, I think,' Peter muttered anxiously. 'Come on.'

They groped their way towards the cliff, only to discover to their dismay that they could no longer find the entrance to the tunnel.

'That's funny. I'm sure it was here,' said Peter.

'Well, we've lost it, that's for sure,' Andrew replied. 'What are we going to do now?'

'Only one thing for it. We'll have to follow the cliff until we come to the beach. Let's just hope these rocks go all the way round and we don't have to swim for it,' Peter answered.

'I feel a bit scared,' Sarah confessed. 'It feels really odd, this mist. Who'd have thought it—in the middle of summer?' She shivered.

'Well, never mind that. Let's just get going,' her elder brother replied, more brusquely than he intended. He, too, felt uneasy.

So they began to scramble across the rocks, keeping as close to the cliff wall as they could. Andrew went in front. Suddenly he gave a shout.

'Hey, you two. I think I've found it. Look.'

His brother and sister caught him up. They were expecting to see the beach but instead he was pointing through the mist to a hole in the cliff face.

'It's the tunnel,' cried Sarah. 'Thank goodness for that.'

'Are you sure?' Peter said. 'I thought it was somewhere back there.'

'So did I,' she replied. 'But you do lose your sense of direction in fog, don't you?'

'I suppose so. Oh, well, at least we're safe now,' he answered. 'You lead the way, Andrew. It might not be so foggy when we reach the top of the cliff.'

The three children groped in single file along the tunnel. The mist was so dense that it was impossible to see the other end. In fact, it was billowing towards them like a cloud of white smoke and in a matter of seconds they had completely lost sight even of one another. It was very odd and a bit scary, like a strange dream.

Andrew stumbled blindly forwards. He thought he should have reached the end of the tunnel by now and felt for the side of the round hole. But he never found it. Instead, to his amazement, he suddenly discovered he was tramping across a pebbly beach. He turned round to look for his brother and sister, but he got the shock of his life as they emerged from the fog.

'Hey, w...what's happened to your clothes?' he stammered. 'And ... and w...where are we?'

Peter and Sarah stopped dead in their tracks. In the thinning mist, all three stared first at each other then at themselves. Gone were their summer togs. Instead, each was clothed in a drab, coarse tunic and breeches, with knee-high leather boots.

Sarah's head swirled and she suddenly felt faint. She grabbed Peter's shoulder for support. 'Oh no! Do you think it's happened again?' she gasped.

Her brother nodded grimly. 'I thought something odd was going on when the mist came in like that. We've been transported into Oswain's world again, I reckon.'

'Don't say we're going to meet another Hagbane,' wailed Sarah. 'I couldn't stand that. Why've we been sent? Where are we? I don't think I want to be here.'

'Oh, shush,' said Andrew. 'It was all right last time—in the end. And we'll probably meet all our old friends. I bet it's a reunion party or something.'

'There's only one way to find out,' said Peter, 'and that's to take a look around. Come on, let's get off this beach for a start. But keep your eyes open for trouble.'

The others nodded and they began to slog their way up the beach. Eventually they could make out the dim outline of trees through the mist and they made for these. That was where they came across an old inn whose faded creaky sign proclaimed it to be *The Seagull.*

'I think we'd better be careful,' Peter cautioned. 'It doesn't look a very pleasant place to me. You keep watch and I'll have a scout round.'

Creeping around the side of the low stone building, he found himself beneath an open window. Cautiously, he peered into the gloomy, smoke-laden bar-room. It was crowded with unsavoury looking seafarers, but what immediately made him duck down was the fact that two of them were sitting deep in conversation right by the open window. He could hear every word they were saying.

'So, y've got the princess, 'ave yer, Jed?'

'Aye, Cap'n Gaspar, sir. That I 'ave. Locked in the outhouse she is. Pretty little thing she be. But got a temper, too. Fair bit my finger she did.'

The other gave a coarse laugh.

'Never mind that, lad. Long as ye've got 'er and the jewel, 'is Eminence'll be right pleased. He'll soon sort 'er temper out and no mistake!'

'Aye, sir, that 'e will. Tell truth, 'e scares me somethin' awful.'

The captain grunted. 'But 'e pays well, Jed, lad. That's what matters. So soon as I've supped me ale, we'll be off with 'er. Round up the crew, lad. We're in fer a fine reward for today's work.'

Peter had heard enough—so this was why they'd

31

been transported here! He hurried back to his brother and sister and quickly recounted what he had overheard.

'Then we must rescue her at once,' exclaimed Sarah. 'Where's this outhouse or whatever it is? Come on!'

'Okay. But let's be careful. They look very nasty types to me and we don't want to get caught.'

The mist was thickening again, so it took them some time to find their way about, but at last they spied the dim outline of a small building. They were just about to creep up to it when a shrill scream pierced the mist, followed by some muffled noises.

'It must be the princess,' cried Peter. 'Quickly!'

The three children hounded across to the outhouse, but only to find the door hanging open and the place empty.

'Which way did they go, d'you think?' Andrew panted.

'Well, it must be towards the sea, so let's follow that path down to the beach,' suggested Peter. He pointed to a narrow track through the grass.

They hastened along it, though by now the mist was so thick that they could scarcely see in front of their faces. At length they came to a point where three paths crossed.

'Now what do we do?' groaned Andrew. 'They could have gone anywhere.'

'I wish someone was here to help us,' said Sarah miserably.

'Hey, look!' cried Peter. 'Over there.'

The others turned to follow his gaze. There in the mist stood the shadowy figure of an old country shepherd. He was pointing with his crook down one of the paths. After hesitating a few moments, they ran across to him. But he instantly vanished before their startled eyes.

'It was a mirage,' declared Andrew.

'It's help,' retorted Sarah. 'Elmesh or somebody must be trying to guide us.' She felt much happier at the thought. 'Come on then. This is the path.'

Peter and Andrew were still uncertain, but Sarah was already away, so they raced after her down the track until they were a few metres from the beach. The mist was more patchy here and before them they could see a longboat floating close to land with the oarsmen at the ready. Two men on the shore were holding someone who, in spite of her clothes, they took to be the princess. A number of barrels and boxes stood nearby awaiting stowage. The children hid behind these.

'Now what do we do?' whispered Andrew. 'We can hardly take that lot on. And we've got no magic weapons, have we?'

'I don't know,' replied Peter. 'Shall we create a diversion or something?'

'Whatever we do, we'll have to be quick. Look, the boat's landing,' said Sarah. 'They'll have her aboard in next to no time.'

The children's problem was resolved for them sooner than they expected. Three pairs of rough hands suddenly seized them from behind. They struggled fiercely, but to no avail. Their captors dragged them relentlessly down towards the sea.

Princess Alena turned to see what the rumpus was about. She was surprised to spy the three children and wondered whether they were from royal families as well.

But before she could think further, somebody came swaggering out of the mist dressed in a dilapidated captain's uniform and carrying a walking stick. He strode up to the princess.

'Well, well, me hearties, what 'ave we here?' He addressed the princess with mock politeness. 'A princess! Allow me to introduce m'self, your majesty. Cap'n Gaspar's the name and I be at your service, ma'am.' He grinned through broken yellowed teeth. 'I request the pleasure of your company aboard me ship.'

Chapter Four

ON BOARD *GRIMWOLF*

Princess Alena turned her head away from the captain. 'I do not accept your offer,' she said haughtily.

He gave a disdainful sniff. 'Have it your own way, then. But you're coming, whether you like it or not!' He turned to Peter, Sarah and Andrew with a gleam in his eye. 'And who might you be, may I ask? You friends of 'ers?'

'Found 'em spying, Cap'n,' explained one of their captors.

'Spyin', eh? Fifty lashes each from the yardarm for that, I reckon. What've yer got to say fer y'selves?'

The children stood in stubborn silence.

'Well, we'll loosen your tongues later. And if we don't, 'is Eminence certainly will. Tide won't wait for us now. Take 'em aboard, men.'

And with that, the princess and the children were bundled into the longboat and rowed out to sea.

Peter peered over the prow as the boat bobbed through the breakers and into open water. Through the mist, he could make out a full-masted galleon riding at anchor in the swell. In spite of their danger, Peter felt a thrill at the thought of being taken aboard what must be a real pirate ship. Andrew joined him.

'Gosh, look at that! Can you see what she's called?'

'No, not yet. It's still too misty.'

They had not long to wait for, with much creaking of oars and grunting by the sailors, the boat rapidly drew near until they could make out the rigging and the name of the ship quite clearly. Painted in blood-red letters on the prow was the single word *Grimwolf*. The figurehead beneath the bowsprit reflected the name—a ghastly wolf's head with blood dripping from its fangs.

Once alongside, the party was quickly transferred to the ship and the four captives were thrown into a cabin beneath the forecastle. Almost immediately the sails were unfurled, the anchor weighed and *Grimwolf* got under way.

'Well, here we are,' said Andrew. 'Now what?'

He looked around the cabin. Aside from a table, a jug of water and some piles of straw, there was nothing. The only light came from a barred window set in the door. It would not be a comfortable trip, he thought.

'We'd better introduce ourselves,' Sarah whispered to her brothers.

Peter addressed the princess. 'Hallo. I'm Peter, and this is my sister Sarah and my brother Andrew.'

'I'm Alena,' she replied sullenly from the corner.

'Hallo,' said the other two.

Sarah sat down beside the princess. 'You're a princess, aren't you? We overheard the pirates speaking, or at least Peter did.'

She nodded glumly. 'A lot of good it's doing me now, isn't it?'

'Why have they kidnapped you?' Andrew asked. 'Is it for a ransom or something?'

'I suppose so,' she answered. 'But I can't understand how they knew who I was. Nobody followed us. No one even knew.'

Prodded by their questions, she proceeded to tell them all that had happened since leaving the palace.

'You shouldn't really have run away, should you?' said Peter when she was through.

'That's my business,' she replied hotly. 'I'm a princess so I can do as I please. How was I to know this was going to happen to me? And what's happened to Crow? And . . . and where are they taking me? They have no right . . .' A stab of pain shot through her head, which made her wince and then burst into tears.

Sarah put her arms around the princess. 'Don't worry, Alena. We'll get out of it somehow. I just know we will.' There was more conviction in her words than in her heart.

Before they could say more the cabin door was flung open and in strode Captain Gaspar with his henchman, Jed. The children retreated into the corner. Jed grabbed Peter and dragged him before the captain who addressed him roughly. 'Now then, laddie, I'll not take nonsense from you. What were you doing spyin' on us? Answer me now, or Jed's liable to get a bit rough. What's yer business?'

Peter remained silent. The captain nodded to Jed who immediately twisted the boy's arm behind his back causing him to cry out in pain.

Sarah was incensed. She hurled herself at the pirate. 'Leave him alone, you bully,' she cried. 'I'll tell you what happened.'

Captain Gaspar motioned Jed to let Peter go. 'Well, a real spitfire and no mistake,' he grinned through his dirty teeth. 'I like a wench with a bit o' spirit. So let's hear you now.'

'We're here 'cos we arrived on the beach and got lost in the mist. So we found our way to *The Seagull*.

That's where we overheard your wicked plans. So we decided to try and rescue the princess. And I think you're very, very evil people,' she finished breathlessly.

Captain Gaspar roared with laughter. 'So that's it, is it? Well, you silly brats, you've got y'selves into trouble, haven't you? 'Cos you're going to have to come along with the princess now. 'Is Eminence will sort out what to do with you. But I don't fancy your chances much.

'Come on, Jed. We'll leave 'em to stew. Teach 'em to meddle in things that be none of their business.'

With that the door was locked and the children left alone.

'Is it really true what you said?' asked Princess Alena.

'Well, yes, it is really,' Sarah replied, wondering how she could explain about the round hole. She thought it better that the pirates didn't know about that.

Princess Alena gave a watery smile. She spoke in a friendly way now. 'Well, thank you for trying. I'm only sorry I've got you into all this. Goodness knows how we'll fare now.'

They sat in brooding silence for a while.

'Hey,' cried Andrew suddenly. 'What city did you say you came from?'

'Elmar,' replied the princess.

'B. . .b. . .but, isn't that Oswain's city?'

'You know Oswain?'

'Why, yes,' chorused the children.

She sat silent for a moment, then said quietly, 'Oswain is my brother.'

Peter, Sarah and Andrew were quite amazed by this news, and all gabbled at once. It took them the best part of an hour to recount all their previous adventures. The hardest part was explaining how they had come from another realm and they were far from convinced that the princess fully believed them. She had hardly ever seen Oswain in any case and didn't have a very high opinion of him, which Sarah found hard to understand.

Nevertheless, this knowledge greatly cheered their spirits, so much so that when Jed came in with food and drink during early evening, he was taken aback to find his captives laughing and joking together.

That night, as they slept on the piles of straw, Sarah dreamt.

In her dream she was feeling her way through a white cloud. Her outstretched hand searched the mist, though she did not know for what. Moments later, she found herself in a dark cavern piled high with treasure. She walked towards a door which opened of its own accord, and there hung a resplendent gem which entranced her with its silvery-blue beauty.

Then, to her horror, a green claw grasped the stone, crushing its light. She wrestled to prevent this, but was instantly surrounded by a pack of howling wolves. With a shriek she ran . . . and ran . . . down an endless black tunnel, pursued by the wild creatures. She felt her heart bursting and could go on no further when before her stood the old shepherd. She ran right on into him . . . and then her dream ended. She awoke. Shivery morning light was just beginning to penetrate the small window.

It was not long before the others awoke and she told them her dream. They puzzled over its meaning until Andrew suddenly smacked his fist into the palm of his hand.

'Got it!' he cried. 'They're after your jewels. That's what it is.'

'No,' said Sarah softly. 'I think it's just one jewel. Have you got something special, Alena?'

The princess hesitated. Then she drew from her bosom the Star-Pearl.

'Do you think it's this?' she asked.

Sarah gazed in wonder at the jewel. 'I'm sure that's what I saw in my . . .'

Just at that moment there was a sound outside and the door began to open.

'Quick, put it away!' urged Peter.

Jed walked in. 'On yer feet,' he commanded. 'No, not you.' He motioned to the princess. 'Only these three. Come on, outside. There's work for the likes of you.'

Reluctantly they left the cabin. For the rest of that morning they were kept busy scrubbing decks and coiling ropes, so that they didn't see the princess again until a cry of 'Land ho!' from the crow's nest told them their journey was at an end.

Coming rapidly into view was a small island not far from the mainland, although far to the south of where the children had been captured. Before long, sailors were scrambling up the rigging and reefing in the sails to the commands of the captain and bosun. The children watched as the vessel drew alongside an empty stone quay and made fast.

The gangplank was dropped and Princess Alena was dragged from her cabin to join the others.

'Come on,' snarled Jed. 'Off yer get.' And he pushed them down on to the quayside. Captain Gaspar followed.

At that moment, a door opened in a small keep at the end of the quay. Before the children's frightened eyes there emerged a grotesque green goblin. And behind him followed a pack of slavering grey wolves.

Sarah screamed.

40

Chapter Five

THE GREY TOWER

Gublak was horribly fat, a monstrosity of squat green flab with sharply pointed ears and cold, calculating eyes which glinted like emeralds. His bald head glistened in the sun, as did the gold chains which hung from his bulging neck and decorated the black kaftan he wore.

As he steadily approached the small group on the quayside time seemed to stand still. An oppressive silence hung over everything. No sailor dared venture down the gangplank to join Captain Gaspar, for they dwelt in dread of the goblin.

'So, you have arrived.' Gublak addressed the captain in a hard, grating voice. He looked first to Sarah and then to Alena. 'Which of these is the princess? And who are these others?' he demanded.

'If it pleases your Eminence, this one is Princess Alena,' the captain answered with respect. 'And these three we caught spyin'. Brought 'em along for your wisdom to judge. Or shall I 'ave 'em killed now, sir?'

'No, fool. I shall see what they are worth first.' He gave an oily smile. 'You have done well, Captain. Better than I expected.'

He reached into his kaftan and drew out a ruby which he tossed to the captain. 'A bonus for you, my friend. The gold you will find in the keep when I have departed. I know your miserable crew will not dare come ashore until then.'

'Your Eminence is most kind,' replied Captain Gaspar as he leered over the ruby in his hand.

Gublak turned to his wolves and addressed the leader of the pack. 'Take them away, Ulris. These three to the kitchens, and the princess—take her to the Grey Tower.'

Ulris snarled and bared his fangs. 'At your bidding, Eminence.'

He fixed his baleful yellow eyes on the captives and they had no option but to obey. Surrounded by the wolves, they stumbled off along the quay while the goblin followed at his own leisurely pace.

Gublak's fortress stood upon the summit of the island at the head of a long winding track. Grey and forbidding it looked, with tall towers and turrets frowning over the forest. The trees stretched away in all directions from the rocky outcrop upon which the fortress stood. The stench of wolves was everywhere and the children's hearts sank as they passed under the gloomy archway which led into the main courtyard. Here they were split up.

'Don't be scared,' shouted Peter after Princess Alena as she was led away. 'We'll think of something, don't you worry.'

She turned and gave him a watery smile. The brief warmth of their companionship made her loneliness all the more bitter.

Peter, Sarah and Andrew were immediately put to work in the basement kitchens where piles of unwashed dishes and sacks of vegetables awaited their attention.

As they toiled they were watched over by lizard-like guards with long tails and scaly skin. They later found out these were called Urgils. Each guard carried a sword, the flat of which was used across the children's shoulders whenever they slacked at their labours or attempted to speak.

All that afternoon they slaved, and it was not until late evening that they were given any food. By the time they were thrown into a dungeon for the night they felt ready to drop.

'Phew! I'm exhausted,' said Andrew as they flopped down.

'Me too,' agreed Sarah. 'What a day. I thought it would never come to an end. I've never seen so much washing up.'

'And don't forget all we did this morning on the ship,' added Andrew. He rolled over to face his brother. 'What are we going to do, Peter?'

'I really don't know,' he replied. 'It looks as though we've been made slaves of that horrible creature, whatever he is. And goodness knows what's happened to Alena. We must try to escape somehow.'

'I do hope she's all right,' said Sarah. 'Do you think it's really that jewel he's after?'

'Can't think what else it can be, can you?' said Peter.

'Then why didn't someone just kill Alena, or at least knock her out, and steal it?' Andrew queried. 'Surely that would've been the easy way?'

'Perhaps it's not as simple as that,' replied his brother.

.   .   *   .   .

Princess Alena, meanwhile, was seated in a large room at the top of a high tower. She was completely alone and the door was locked.

Surprisingly, her prison was comfortably furnished with all that was needed to make her feel at home, and plenty of food had been provided for her to eat. After some initial suspicions that it might be poisoned she had taken the plunge and hungrily scoffed the lot.

Even more astonishing were the elegant clothes which she found in the wardrobe. They were all her size and of even better quality than she was used to wearing back home. She tried some and was particularly pleased with a silvery-white gown which she decided to keep on for a while. Perhaps this adventure was going to turn out all right after all. At least she was being treated as a princess should be.

But then her mind went back to her newly found friends. Whatever would become of them? And she was a prisoner herself, however nice the room was. She paced to and fro across the floor.

'Why doesn't anyone come for me?' she muttered. 'What does that ugly creature want, anyway?'

She felt the Star-Pearl about her neck. 'Well, he's not having this, that's for sure. It belongs to me and me alone. So there!'

She gazed out of the windows. The view was stunning. Not only could she see the courtyards and battlements of the castle below, but the whole expanse of the forested island and the blue sea beyond. In one direction she could make out the hazy outline of a mountainous coastline. She wondered where it was.

At long last, as the sun was setting and an ominous green mist was rising from the trees, there came the sudden rattle of a key in the door. She sat on the bed gripping the covers tightly as the door opened. One of the Urgils entered.

'His Eminence requires your presence at his table,'

44

he said briefly. 'You are to accompany me now.'

Knowing it was pointless to argue, and curious to discover what was to happen, Princess Alena allowed herself to be escorted down the stairs. They passed along many corridors lit with burning torches until they reached a pair of large doors flanked by two guards. At a sign from her escort the doors were swung open and she was ushered into a spacious hall.

Before her stood Gublak, and beyond she could see a table heavily laden with food. A fire burned brightly upon a massive hearth, casting flickering shadows around the walls.

'Ah, welcome, Princess Alena.' His voice possessed a silky quality, but she knew it concealed malice. There was no mistaking those eyes. 'I see you have found garments more becoming for a princess. I trust they are to your liking. Won't you please join me for dinner?'

'I don't know who you are,' she replied coldly, 'but I've been kidnapped, maltreated, and brought here without any explanation whatsoever. I am extremely cross and require you to release both me and my companions this very instant.'

Her face grew very red and she clenched her fists angrily.

'Forgive me, dear Princess. I will explain everything. But first let me introduce myself. My name is Gublak, and I am the ruler of this island. However, you will have realized by now that my power extends far beyond its shores.

'As to the reason I have brought you here—you have something that I want, something I dearly desire.' His eyes glittered greedily and she shrank back with distaste. 'You see,' he went on, 'I am a collector of beautiful things. I have amassed treasures more than you can imagine, vast caverns of gold, silver and rolled parchment scroll tied with red ribbon.

'This, Master, is all you require,' he cawed.

Gublak took the scroll and unfurled it.

'Excellent, excellent,' he muttered as his greedy green eyes scanned the contents. 'The Star-Pearl is within our grasp.'

jewels. Works of art that would dazzle you. These bring me great satisfaction—but, alas, beautiful as they are, they are lifeless. There is no *real* power in gold.

'But *you* have something more,' he continued. 'You possess the Star-Pearl of Elmar. That is what I most desire.'

'The Star-Pearl is mine,' she replied steadily, though her heart was thumping hard. 'I'm not prepared to give it up.'

Gublak smirked. 'We shall see. I am very rich and am prepared to pay a great price for this jewel. You could be a very wealthy princess, you know, and wield great power with the treasures I would bestow upon you for this . . . this trinket. It could be all yours to do with as you pleased. Just think of it.'

'The Star-Pearl is not for sale,' she replied shortly. 'That's all there is to it. Now let me go back to my room while you plan how you are going to return me to the mainland.'

The goblin glared angrily at her determined face. 'Very well. For the moment, that is how I shall leave it. But first, there is something I must put to the test. Guards!'

The two Urgils rushed in.

'You, seize her,' he commanded one of them.

Before the princess could move, her arms were firmly pinioned behind her back. Gublak spoke to the other guard.

'Remove that jewel which hangs about her neck.'

Princess Alena fought vainly, lashing out with her feet as the scaly creature approached, but to no avail. His claw took hold of the chain and he lifted the jewel from her dress. But, the moment he laid his hand upon the Star-Pearl itself a sigh like an endless sadness escaped his jaws, and he fell dead at her feet.

The other guard released her immediately and sprang back, while the princess stared horror-struck at the fallen creature.

'Then the rumour is true,' muttered Gublak. 'No matter, no matter.' To the remaining Urgil he ordered, 'Return the princess to the tower and lock her in securely.'

Princess Alena sat in bed an hour later with a certain satisfaction in her heart. She fingered the Star-Pearl with an affection which she had not felt before.

'Hm,' she thought. 'He won't try that again in a hurry. I feel sorry about the guard, but that's not really my fault. Perhaps there's more power in this than I thought. Maybe things will turn out all right after all.'

And with that she lay down to sleep.

But it was not to be a pleasant night for Princess Alena. The moment her head touched the pillow it began to throb. Her mind was filled with the image of the crystal ball in the gypsy caravan and try as she might she could not shut it out. Weird voices began to jabber again. She broke into a cold sweat and tossed and turned in her bed. A cool wind whistled through the windows, blowing the curtains into wildly contorted shadows. Things fell. The room span. At times she thought there were people walking around. She heard strange scurrying noises and couldn't tell whether they were in her head or under the bed. She felt terribly afraid.

Then the wolves began their blood chilling howls from far below. Shivering, she clutched at the bedclothes and wished for the dawn.

In his room Gublak smiled grimly as he sat, fingertips touching beneath his chin. 'Stubborn she may be, but we'll see what a night in the Grey Tower will do about that!' he mused to himself.

Chapter Six

THE CUNNING GOBLIN

Peter, Sarah and Andrew were all awake very early the next morning. They felt extremely stiff after the labours of the previous day and a night on hard wooden bunks.

'Oof, my arms don't half ache,' said Andrew.

'It's my back,' groaned Sarah as she sat up gingerly. 'How are you, Peter?'

'Hm, not too bad, I think.' He staggered to his feet. 'Ouch! I spoke too soon. My knees hurt.'

'It's all that deck scrubbing,' retorted Andrew.

They spent the next few minutes stretching and stumbling around their cell trying to ease the aches and pains. But the thought of another day in the kitchens made them feel even worse.

'Look, we've just got to escape from this place somehow. I don't fancy being a slave for the rest of my life,' said Peter.

'Nor me,' declared Andrew. 'Anybody got any ideas?' He heaved at the bars on the window. 'No chance here, they're solid as a rock.'

'That would be too good to be true,' his brother commented. 'Anyway, it wouldn't help much. We've got to get Alena out as well, and we don't even know where she is.'

'The Grey Tower that creature said—wherever that is,' said Sarah. 'I wonder if she's still got that pearl?'

'If that's what he's really after,' Andrew challenged.

'Well, I don't think it can be anything else,' Sarah retorted. 'I'm sure my dream was right.'

'You and your dreams.'

Sarah looked cross and Peter intervened before they could start squabbling. 'Come on, you two. This isn't going to help. What we really need to do is keep our eyes peeled today and see if we can find an escape route. Let's hope we can contact Alena as well.'

His brother and sister agreed and apologized to each other.

A guard came for them shortly afterwards and led them away to the kitchens where they were allowed to wash and have breakfast before being set to work.

.   .   *   .   .

Dawn came as a mighty relief to Princess Alena. Never had she known a night like the one which had just passed. Though she must have dozed at times, she felt as if she had not slept at all. She stared mournfully in the mirror at the dark shadows under her eyes.

'Ugh, what a sight!' she exclaimed. 'I don't want to go through that again.' She shuddered at the memory of the past hours.

But morning light often fills the fearful with fresh courage, and she set her jaw firmly.

'He's not going to get me that way,' she declared. She ignored the dresses in the wardrobe and deliberately donned her old peasant's garb, then sat waiting to see what would happen. It was not long before the guard came and took her again to Gublak.

The goblin looked at her with half-amusement as she shambled into the room.

'Good morning. I trust you slept well,' he said.

'No I didn't and you know jolly well I didn't,' she snapped.

'I am sorry to hear that,' he lied. 'Maybe I can offer you breakfast to make amends?'

Princess Alena hesitated a moment, then glanced at the well-stocked table. She was hungry, so with a curt nod and not another word she helped herself to the food. Gublak watched her in silence.

While she was on her last piece of toast he started to talk again. He sat near the fireplace staring into the distance.

'Last night I offered you vast wealth in exchange for the Star-Pearl, yet you refused to part with it. I must say I was surprised at your foolish reluctance— without which, by the way, one of my guards would not have died.'

The princess looked up at him sharply. 'I was sorry about that. But it was hardly my fault, was it? You should not have tried to steal it. Why do you want the Star-Pearl, anyway? You're obviously rich. What's so special about this?'

He turned slowly to face her. His green eyes glittered and seemed to bore right into hers.

'You appear to know very little about the treasure you carry,' he said quietly. 'Deep mysteries and powers are hidden in the depths of its light. One such as I could unlock those secrets. That is why I wish to gaze upon it, to understand it, to . . . '

'You mean you wish to use it for your own ends,' she interrupted.

'Oh, yes, if you mean there is power in knowledge,' he breathed. 'But what is so wrong with that? After all, you had power when you were a princess.'

'Yes, but mine wasn't . . . isn't evil.'

The goblin shrugged. 'What is evil and what is good? I treat my servants well and I am generous with my favours. When I possess the Star-Pearl I shall be even more lavish towards those who serve me. Surely you are being evil by not letting me do that?'

The princess did not know how to reply. She was silent for a moment. Then she blurted out, 'I think what you're saying is a lot of nonsense. And you're still not having it.'

She walked over to the fire and stood warming her hands. Without turning she asked, 'Why don't you just kill me? Then you could have it, couldn't you?'

'Alas, you know that is not possible,' he replied with a sigh. 'The moment you were to die, the Star-Pearl would simply vapourize and be lost for ever.'

This was news to the princess but she didn't let on. It gave her considerable comfort to know that whatever else happened, Gublak would not dare let her die. Such information might well prove useful.

The goblin decided to change his approach. 'Why do you cling on to this jewel? Why is it so important to you?' he asked. 'I am not sure you even know why you have got it.'

'I've been taught never to give it away,' she said slowly, 'because if I do, I shall cease to be a princess and I shall lose my name.'

Gublak's eyes gleamed. 'What utter rubbish!' he cried scornfully. 'Superstitious nonsense. As if your name depended on that!'

Princess Alena turned on him hotly. 'Well, that's what I've been told. Why should I believe otherwise?'

'My dear child, has it never occurred to you that your name is what *you* call yourself? It does not exist just because of your birthstone. If that is all it does for you, you might as well sell it straight away.'

His words touched something in the princess. She felt confused. 'I . . . I . . . don't know about that.'

Gublak followed through quickly.

'Look, I admire your independence—the way you ran away from home to choose your own life. That is the mark of a real princess. It has nothing to do with this . . . this Star-Pearl. You could prove the truth of my words simply by removing it now. In fact, that would show even more how much of a princess you really are.'

The goblin's persuasive tongue was having its effect. Princess Alena moved quietly to the window and stared out over the courtyard below for a long time.

.   .   *   .   .

The Urgils were not so strict that day and the children found they could whisper at times. Also, while they were carrying out their chores they were beginning to get some idea of the layout of their part of the fortress. The kitchens proved to be only one short flight of steps below the main courtyard. This was surrounded by a covered walkway off which were several entrances into other parts of the castle. The square was overlooked by many windows and lofty towers.

All this the children observed when they were marched up the steps and across to a side gate. From there they were ordered to carry provisions into the castle from wagons which journeyed to and from

Grimwolf throughout the day.

In an unguarded moment on his way up from the kitchens Andrew seized his opportunity to slip away and spy out the land. He ducked behind the low wall which supported the colonnades of the covered walkway. Keeping down, but peering about occasionally, he crept down the courtyard.

He had not gone far when he spotted a movement at one of the first floor windows. To his joy he recognized Princess Alena. Would she see him? Throwing caution to the wind he stood and waved. For a moment there was no response. Then she spotted him. He saw her hand give a surreptitious little flutter in answer.

Just then he heard the angry shout of an Urgil who was scuttling across towards him. The guard dragged him by his ear back to work and Andrew received quite a few blows for his courage. But he'd found out something very important. They knew now that the princess was not kept permanently locked in the tower.

Princess Alena's heart leapt when she saw Andrew. His eager wave gave her new hope. She was sad when he was caught so quickly, but it filled her with fresh determination. She turned on Gublak.

'I want my friends released,' she demanded. 'You've no right to keep them like slaves.'

The wily goblin blinked but was not thrown off balance.

'But of course,' he replied smoothly, 'though "friends" is rather a grand term for children you hardly know, isn't it? Commoners at that. Nevertheless, they will be released—the moment you hand over the Star-Pearl. Otherwise, they remain victims of your, um, selfishness, don't they?'

She shrugged her shoulders. 'You're wasting your

time. I'm not going to let you have it and that's that. So what happens now? Are you going to lock me up again?'

'Why, no. As a princess you are perfectly free to roam the grounds. You shall not try to escape, of course, nor make any contact with those commoners. But I wish you to enjoy my hospitality. It is, after all, the least one member of royalty can do for another.'

Princess Alena shuddered at this comparison between Gublak and herself.

'I will see you at lunch,' he went on. 'And, please,' he gave a disdainful glance at her frock, 'do try to dress as is becoming for a princess!'

Later, she sat alone on a wall in the garden and gazed upon the Star-Pearl. The beautiful blue light twinkled in its depths and she felt strangely encouraged by its glow. But then other lights flashed in her head and her eyes began to sting. She wiped them, and the Star-Pearl seemed to grow very dull. She heaved a great sigh and replaced it in her bosom.

After lunch, Gublak took her on a tour of his treasure stores. Somewhat in two minds, she had nevertheless dressed herself in one of the gowns which he had provided for her. She had chosen a stunning blue creation and Gublak had sounded appreciative.

He had not in the least exaggerated his wealth. The sheer quantities of treasure left her quite breathless. Gold seemed to drip from the walls and spill over the floors of the vaults. Gemstones glittered from all directions—fiery rubies, cool sapphires, sparkling diamonds and many others she hardly recognized.

'Of course, you are used to this sort of thing,' the goblin said airily.

'Oh, yes,' replied the princess without much

conviction. The truth was that she was given very little access to the royal treasures back home. Something about 'when she was old enough'. In any case, she doubted whether the palace had anything like this kind of wealth.

Gublak encouraged her to play with the treasures. She tried on coronets, smothered her fingers with jewelled rings, hung dozens of solid gold necklaces about her. All the while he flattered her beauty and 'wise choices'. He told her she seemed to be in her natural element.

One thing particularly entranced her. She came across a set of puppets made of gold and silver with gems for eyes and operated by gold wires. The skilful workmanship made them seem almost lifelike.

'Oh, they're beautiful!' she exclaimed. 'Can I play with them for a while?'

'My dear princess, you can play with these and many, many other treasures.' He opened a door revealing a whole room full of such toys. She gasped and made to go in, but he checked her with his arm. 'However, I regret I must say again that the price for all this is one Star-Pearl.'

She turned away sadly and was sullen from then on and would not speak. Gublak smiled to himself.

That evening she was returned to the Grey Tower. All her memories of the previous night came flooding back as she lay trembling in bed. She waited for the terrors of the dark. But they did not come, and soon she was fast asleep.

Yet the evil magic had more than one way of working on her. She dreamed of possessing vast treasures, of having freedom to do whatever she wanted. She imagined travelling the world in a golden coach. At one point she even thought of having Peter, Sarah and Andrew along as friends to share the toys. But then, she was not sure if she knew them well enough or if they would be able to appreciate such things. No, she would have to choose her friends with care; people who would respect that she was a princess because she wanted to be. Maybe Peter and Andrew could be her servants, and Sarah her handmaid. . . .

Her dreams came to an end with a picture of a smiling Gublak ushering her into a vast room of sparkling treasure. In her hand was a golden puppet, while in his hand was a rather dull looking pearl on a silver chain.

Chapter Seven

GUBLAK CHANGES

Much to her surprise, Princess Alena was allowed to breakfast alone the following day. In fact, it was not until mid-morning that Gublak entered the room and found her sitting by the window looking quite forlorn. She heaved a great sigh as he approached but didn't turn to look at him.

'How much are you going to offer me today? Or are you going to browbeat me into selling it?' she asked.

Gublak smiled as he replied, 'On the contrary. I have changed my mind. I no longer wish to buy it.'

The princess shot him a surprised glance, then turned to eye him warily.

'What do you mean?' she demanded. To her annoyance she couldn't avoid the feeling that she was in danger of losing a bargain.

The goblin ambled across to the fire and stood with his back towards it, facing her.

'You appear surprised,' he said. 'Yet should you be? Do you not call yourself a princess? Well, I shall allow you to be one. No longer shall I seek to bribe you into selling me the Star-Pearl. Instead, I wish to propose—a partnership. Perhaps even one day a marriage.'

She stared at him incredulously. Her mouth hung open but no words would come out.

'A . . . a . . . partnership? Marriage? You have to be jesting,' she spluttered at last. 'How on earth could I ever love an ugly creature such as you? Never in a thousand years!'

Gublak was unmoved by her scorn. He came closer and addressed her in slow, deliberate tones.

'They say beauty is in the eye of the beholder. You describe me as ugly, but could it perhaps be that your eyes deceive you? I will demonstrate.'

He stared straight at her while removing something from his pocket. Between bony finger and thumb he held a small glowing glass ball which he slowly circled between his face and hers. The princess felt her head begin to spin and everything became fuzzy. Then her eyes cleared. She gave a start. Before her stood a fine handsome man, suave, smiling and clothed in blue. Of Gublak there was no sign.

'Who . . . who are you?' she stammered. 'What's happened?'

'I am Gublak,' replied the stranger. The voice was unaltered.

'But you can't be!'

'Did I not say that it may have been your eyes which were deceived? Only now are you seeing truly. Before this, you were blinded to the truth by your own twisted thoughts. I am indeed Gublak, and this is how I can appear to you for ever.'

The princess sat back weakly in her chair. She didn't know what to say. She rubbed her eyes in disbelief but still the handsome man remained. He spoke again.

'Freedom and wealth are yours, Alena. But what are they without someone with whom to share them?

You are surely not such a selfish person as to want it all for yourself.

'Yesterday, when you were young, I offered you the ability to make others rich by entrusting me with the Star-Pearl. I no longer ask that, for suddenly you are of age. Instead, O fair princess, I beg you but to share its power with me, so that together we may bring happiness to our subjects.'

His eyes were appealing, his voice gently persuasive. Princess Alena felt very strange and quite grown up all of a sudden. A daring vision of a new life with Gublak flooded her mind.

'With our shared wealth and the power of the Star-Pearl we shall live happily and bring pleasure to many,' he continued. 'You as my princess and I as your prince.'

Alena tried to pull herself together and remember that this was the goblin speaking. But the magic was powerful.

'Yet you still want me to give you the Star-Pearl?' she queried.

He drew back in mock horror. 'Dear princess, I should not ever demand such a thing of you again. All I ask is to gaze upon it from time to time. Should you ever permit me to *borrow* it that would bring me great joy, but I would not force you so to do.'

He gazed earnestly into her eyes.

'Say you will stay. Share my wealth. Be my princess.'

She groped for a reply in the face of his charm.

'B. . .b. . .but I'm already a princess in my own country. Surely I should return to my home?'

He looked downcast.

'Why should you leave? After all, did you not choose to run away, to find adventure? And have you not found it? You chose your path and it has turned

59

out for the good. Why go back?'

'I don't know why I ran away,' she replied slowly. 'I'm very confused about all that.' She looked at him and felt very weak. 'I . . . I must think about what you say.'

'Of course, my dear,' the handsome figure replied. 'I shall leave you now to consider my offer.'

He walked towards the door and Alena felt like begging him not to go.

'By the way,' he said from the doorway, 'tonight I have a pleasant surprise for you. Dress well for the occasion.'

And with that he was gone. Alena gave a wistful sigh and wondered what she should do.

.　　.　　*　　.　　.

Peter, Sarah and Andrew awoke that same morning determined to form an escape plan.

'Right,' said Peter. 'First of all, what do we need?'

'Food,' Andrew replied promptly.

'All you ever think about is your stomach,' his sister teased.

'But he's right,' said Peter. 'So we'd better start collecting some today. I think we'll have to find water as we go because we've nothing to carry it in. What else do we need?'

'Some way of getting out of here without being noticed,' said Andrew.

'How about hiding in one of the wagons?' Sarah suggested.

'No, too obvious. Anyway, they're driven by those Urgils. We wouldn't get far,' Peter replied.

'Even if we get away from here, we've still got to get off the island. How are we going to do that?'

Andrew asked.

'I think we've got two choices,' his brother answered. 'Either we find a boat and row across to the mainland. Or we stow away on *Grimwolf*. Either way, we must get down to the harbour without being seen.'

'Or getting caught by those wolves,' Sarah added with a shudder.

The others agreed wholeheartedly but before they could say more the guard came to escort them to the kitchens.

On their arrival they found things very busy. The Urgils were obviously preparing for a big feast and were hurrying backwards and forwards. This resulted in the children being scarcely supervised. They were simply sent into a side room filled with sacks of potatoes and ordered to keep peeling until told to stop.

It was while pulling the second sack from the pile that Andrew made his discovery. Set into the floor was an iron ring. He bent down and gave it a tug. To his delight a small trapdoor swung open revealing a cellar. The children crowded round excitedly and peered into the gloom. The floor was only about two metres below. Peter hesitated but a moment.

'Watch the door, Sarah. I'm going down.'

'All right, but mind how you go. Look out for rats.'

'How are you going to get out again, Pete?' Andrew asked.

He thought for a moment. 'Push one of those sacks of spuds down and I reckon I can reach if I stand on it.'

The other nodded and with that Peter swung himself over the side and dropped with a thud on to the floor beneath. He vanished from his brother's sight but was back half a minute later looking glum.

'Not much luck,' he said. 'It's only a storage cellar. I can't find any other way out. You'd better shove that sack down, Andrew, so I can get up.'

'Pity there's not a secret tunnel like you read about in books,' said Andrew when Peter had clambered back out.

'Hm,' Peter looked about him slowly. 'But it's given me an idea. Look, grab some empty sacks and see what food you can find. Don't forget one for Alena as well. We'll start by hiding it down there. And now, listen. . . .'

He unfolded a daring plan to his brother and sister.

The guards were so lax because of their extra work that Sarah actually managed to slip upstairs for a while during early afternoon. It was then that she spotted Princess Alena wandering across the court-yard lost in thought. With a couple of quick glances around she slipped behind one of the columns and in a stage whisper called to the princess.

'Psst. Alena!'

The princess gave a start and glanced around.

'Over here,' Sarah whispered. 'To your left. Just act natural and sit on the wall.'

Princess Alena followed the voice and obeyed, looking straight ahead.

'Listen, it's me. Sarah. Are you all right, Alena?'

She nodded, then said, 'Yes, but you're taking an awful risk speaking to me. I daren't stay here long.'

'I know,' said Sarah urgently. 'But listen, we've got an escape plan and you'll have to get ready for it. We're going to do it tomorrow. Can you come here in the morning? And can you wear something for travelling in? I won't tell you any more now 'cos I'd better be getting back before I'm missed. Anyway, that horrible creature might get it out of you.'

The princess hesitated before replying.

'I . . . I . . . don't know whether I want to escape,' she said eventually.

Unable to see the confused look on her face Sarah imagined the princess was simply scared. 'Don't be afraid,' she said. 'We'll get away with it, you'll see. Just be here tomorrow. If you can't, we'll wait till the next day, but we'll rescue you somehow.'

And with that she darted back to the kitchens, leaving Princess Alena even more confused and unhappy.

.　　.　　*　　.　　.

The surprise which Gublak had promised took place that evening when Princess Alena was ushered into the great hall. She found it filled with Urgils dressed in their best uniforms. The children were there all spruced up, as was Captain Gaspar and, of course, Gublak himself.

To the princess he still appeared as a handsome prince, though to everyone else he was nothing but the ugly goblin. Princess Alena's heart fluttered as he approached.

'Alena, you look wonderful. Allow me, please, to explain all this.' He gestured around the room. 'I have laid on a party for you to make up for the one you missed on your birthday. I do hope you will enjoy it.'

He turned to the assembled company and made a signal, at which the Urgils gave three cheers and raised their glasses in her honour. Princess Alena didn't know what to say. She flushed with embarrassment. Gublak took her arm and escorted her to a table overflowing with food. Musicians began to play and the feasting began.

Only Peter, Sarah and Andrew looked miserable.

'What's up with Alena?' whispered Andrew. 'Why's she looking so happy with that revolting creature?'

'I don't know,' replied Sarah. 'I just can't understand how she could let him touch her. I'd hate it. Ugh!'

'Look, she's joking with him now,' Andrew observed. 'And . . . and she's showing him the Star-Pearl.'

'Oh, please don't let her give it to him,' cried Sarah.

'She's been entranced,' said Peter grimly, as the memory of his experience with Hagbane flooded into his mind.[1] 'Come on. We've got to interrupt this.'

The children made their way across to the couple.

'Hallo, Alena,' said Peter. 'Happy late birthday. Though it can hardly be happy when we're all kept prisoners here, can it?'

The princess looked irritated at his interruption.

'I think it is very kind of Gublak to do this for me. And actually I'm quite enjoying myself,' she said primly. 'At least, I was until just now.'

Gublak smiled into her eyes. 'I do not think Peter understands, do you? That is the problem with these commoners.'

'I think I understand very well,' Peter exploded. 'You've got Alena under a spell, you evil creature.'

A flicker of emotion flashed across the goblin's face but he remained smiling.

'I do not wish to be rude in the presence of the princess, but it does seem you lack the party spirit, young man. I think you should depart.' He motioned to a guard nearby. 'These commoners are leaving us.

---

[1]See *Hagbane's Doom*, page 27

64

Will you escort them to their quarters?'

A pang of conscience struck Princess Alena and for a moment she knew the truth. In that instant she recalled Sarah's words and resolved to meet them on the following day. But Gublak's spell was so powerful, and she had become so weak, that she could find nothing to say. The children looked back at her with despair as they were led away.

'I have a present for you,' said Gublak immediately they were out of sight.

To her wonder he presented her with a large parcel which, when she opened it with eager fingers, turned out to be the golden puppets she had so desired the day before. Her eyes sparkled with delight, and she thought no more of her friends.

That night Princess Alena dreamt again, and in her dreams she heard the jabbering voices growing louder and louder. Then she saw accusing fingers wagging at her. The voices nagged on and on. She began to recognize them as those of her nanny, her teachers and her parents. Their faces appeared and were angry as they scolded her. It seemed to the princess as if that was all they had ever done. She pressed her hands to her ears and squeezed her eyes shut tight. All she wanted to do was flee from them and have her own life.

Beckoning in the dark was Gublak, tall and handsome, and she found herself running in slow motion towards him. She felt herself about to fall into his outstretched arms.

.   .   *   .   .

While she slept, Gublak had a visitor. It was Crow. He landed upon the table and let fall from his beak a

Chapter Eight

THE SCROLL

Darker powers than either the children or Princess Alena could imagine were at work behind Gublak's greed. It was of little interest to those powers whether or not the goblin came to possess the Star-Pearl, for they knew full well it would never serve the cause of evil. What they dearly desired was that the princess should give it up, for then the royal line of the West would break and she herself would serve their wicked purposes.

This Oswain perceived, many miles distant, as he sat once more by Elmere in the enchanted glade of the Great Forest. Aged Trotter was with him.

'The dark powers seek only to destroy the noble and pure.' Oswain spoke gravely. 'In their wickedness they seek to make the innocent like themselves. They seize any opportunity, find any chink in the armour. I suspect Alena has long been watched for such a moment as this.'

The old badger replied with quiet wisdom. 'Yet darkness is not the whole truth, my friend. Indeed, one day it shall be revealed as but a passing lie. The pure love of Elmesh rules for ever, serene as El-la itself.'

They both gazed into the night sky at the star so

named and felt its wondrous power.

'You speak truth as always, Trotter,' Oswain smiled. 'Hope there is indeed. Yet love must be freely offered by Elmesh's subjects and evil freely rejected. Alena will be tested as to her true desires; she must choose, and no help may be given which takes away that choice.'

'Yet some aid they may receive this day, I think,' Trotter answered. 'For I feel in my bones that much will happen ere the sun sets.'

'Then to this end we must bend what energies we may possess,' Oswain replied.

.   .   *   .   .

Princess Alena had been unsure what to wear the next morning. On the one hand she now wished to please Gublak but on the other she wanted to be suitably attired for a possible escape. In the end she chose a smart leather jerkin and trousers and boots to go with a frilly white blouse.

Gublak did not look quite as handsome when he walked in after she had breakfasted, but this barely registered with her. What caught her attention at once was the large, black bird accompanying him. She leapt to her feet.

'Crow!' she cried. 'Where have you been? What are you doing here?'

'Good morning, Mistress,' he cawed in response and cocked his head towards Gublak.

But before the goblin could say anything realization dawned on Alena's face, quickly to be replaced by a look of fury.

'It was you!' she exclaimed. 'You led me into the trap. You horrible traitor! And I trusted you. . . .'

For a moment she was beside herself with rage and the bird cowered behind Gublak, fearing she might tear him wing from wing.

The goblin raised a steadying hand. He spoke gently. 'My dear Alena, believe me it was necessary. If there had been another way less distressing to you, we would have used it.'

'Don't try to get round me like that,' she cried. 'I see it all clearly now. Crow is in your employ. He was your tool to get me here and persuade me to part with my Star-Pearl. Well, that's that. I shall never give in to you. Do you hear? Never! And I can see you for what you are, you ugly, fat, green goblin!'

Sharp pains stabbed her mind at that moment. She sat down clutching her head and burst into tears. Gublak and Crow waited until her sobbing subsided. The latter spoke.

'Mistress, what you say is true, but not all the truth. If I had not acted as I did, something awful would have remained hidden from you until, when you found out, it would have been too late.'

'What Crow says is correct,' continued Gublak. 'When I offered to purchase the Star-Pearl from you it was because I already knew it was worthless to you. But then I felt pity and love. I desired to share my wealth and reign with you because . . .' he paused, 'because otherwise you would have nothing.'

'What do you mean? I don't know what you're talking about,' she snivelled. 'I have plenty of things at home.'

The goblin shook his head pityingly, then looked her straight in the eye. 'You have no idea, have you? Then I must reveal the painful truth to you, Alena. I am afraid you were not born a princess at all.'

A stunned silence greeted his words. Princess Alena's mind whirled. This was the last thing she had expected to hear.

'You're lying,' she eventually whispered, though without much conviction.

'Unfortunately not,' Gublak replied solemnly. He drew from his robe the rolled parchment and laid it on the table before her. 'Read this for yourself.'

Hesitantly, she unrolled it and read:

> In the seven hundredth year from the foundation of Elmar, being also the first glorious year of Oswain's rule over the Great Forest in the Eastern Lands, a girl-child of unknown name and parentage is hereby adopted by their royal personages, the King and Queen of the Wester Lands, resident in the royal city of Elmar, to be known henceforth as Alena, that is Star-born.

It was signed by the Clerk to the Royal Court and had the official seal. There was no doubt that it was genuine.

The information hit the princess like a thunderbolt. She dropped the scroll and stared blankly at the table as her world fell apart. 'Of unknown name and parentage. . . .' She was not really a princess at all. She was a nobody.

For all these years she had been made to live a lie. The airs and graces, the palace life, the clothes, they were all a sham. How she had tried to impress Gublak with her royal blood, when all along he knew the truth. What a fool she felt! Why had nobody ever told her before? She was shattered.

Gublak was speaking again.

'You understand now that the Star-Pearl is but a useless charm. It cannot make you a princess when you are not. What value is a Star-Pearl to one who is not really Star-born?'

'What can I do?' groaned the princess in despair. 'I

have no name of my own. No real parents. I've lost everything. Oh, why did you have to tell me this?'

'All is not lost,' replied Gublak. 'For have I not said you can choose to be a princess. I offer you the opportunity to do that. You may not have been born a princess, but you have shown the qualities of a ruler. By running away from home you have chosen your own pathway and fate has led you to me who can give you wealth and power. This you have earned on your own. You need no Star-Pearl. Let us put its powers to other uses, by all means, but let it not bind you to a false past any longer.'

'You can have it for all I care,' she said morosely. 'What is the point of keeping it?'

Her words were like music in Gublak's ears. His greedy eyes lit up and he rubbed his spiny fingers together in eager anticipation. His hands stretched towards her neck.

'Do you really mean that?' he breathed.

But the evil in Gublak had gone too far in its desire to conquer. Princess Alena glanced up just as his hands reached for the silver chain. In that moment she saw the endless depths of greed in his bleak soul. His eyes, hard and cruel, were filled only with intense craving. They frightened her and she drew back with a shudder.

'I . . . I . . . do, but not quite at this moment,' she stammered. 'I need a little time to think, to be alone. This has been a great shock to me.'

The goblin looked disappointed but quickly shrugged it off. 'But of course. Though let it not be too long. I would have you enjoy your privileges as my princess, after all.'

'Then I'll take a walk now if you don't mind,' she replied and rose shakily to her feet. Gublak and Crow watched as she left the room.

'Do not worry, Master. There is no fight left in her. What will you do with her once the Star-Pearl is yours?'

'I have not decided,' the goblin replied. 'I may have her killed, or she may be useful to me in some way. We shall see. Either way, it will not be long now.'

Out in the courtyard Princess Alena anxiously looked about her. There was no sign of Sarah. Round and round she strolled, then, aware that Gublak and Crow might be watching from the windows, she made to pass through one of the gates leading into other parts of the fortress, but instead ducked behind the low wall, as Andrew had done. She crept along until she reached the corner, then got the shock of her life as Sarah's face appeared from the other side so quickly that they almost bumped noses. She scarcely stifled a scream.

'Shush,' urged Sarah and squeezed her hand. 'Well done. Come on, this way.'

Princess Alena hesitated.

'What's wrong?' asked Sarah.

'I don't know,' she replied. 'I don't know what to do.'

She rapidly tried to explain what had happened to her.

'Listen,' Sarah said when she had finished. 'This is all too much for me. But all I know is that that goblin, Gublak or whatever he calls himself, is evil and if he gets his hands on your Star-Pearl something terrible will occur. You mustn't let that happen. You've got to come with us, Alena.'

'I suppose so,' the princess replied. 'But what's the point? I don't know who I am any longer. I feel I want to give up.'

'But that's what he's trying to make you feel,' Sarah insisted. 'Now come on, before somebody catches us.'

With great reluctance Princess Alena followed Sarah around the wall and downstairs into the corridor leading to the kitchens, where they were met by Andrew.

'Quick, in here,' he urged and shoved the princess without ceremony into the potato store room. He pulled the trapdoor open.

'Down you go. It's all right. It's quite safe.'

She hesitated a moment before obeying. Andrew followed and closed the door. They were only just in time, for a guard came past and demanded from Sarah where she had been.

'I can't see my brother Andrew anywhere,' she said truthfully.

The guard dragged her into the main kitchen where Peter was tidying up the firewood and demanded, 'Where is the other one?'

'He's not in here,' answered Peter. 'In fact, come to think of it, I haven't seen him for quite a while.'

The guard uttered a curse. 'That little trouble-maker's run off again. Just wait till I get my claws on him.' He called to the other guard who was on kitchen duty. 'Hey, Gurk, that brat's on the run again. Come on, we'd better catch 'im before 'is Eminence finds out.' He turned to Peter and Sarah. 'And don't you try anything funny while we're gone.'

The children nodded innocently, but as soon as the Urgils had gone they began to rush about. Sarah spread old sacks everywhere and scattered firewood while Peter heaved a large barrel of oil on to its side so that it ran all over the wooden floor. They ladled more oil on to the tables and splashed it over the walls.

'This had better work,' muttered Peter. 'You ready, Sarah?'

She nodded and ran to the door. Her brother took

73

a burning brand from the fireplace and joined her. Then he touched a piece of oil-soaked sacking with the flame. For one instant nothing happened. Then the oil caught. They watched for a few seconds as the flames spread, then darted into the adjacent potato room. Peter wrenched open the trapdoor and Sarah held it at an angle while he manoeuvred a sack of potatoes across the lid so that it would be hidden once it was closed. Then they both slipped down to join Andrew and the princess.

Flames ran across the floor and licked up the walls. Within minutes the kitchen was a roaring inferno. Wooden beams crackled and sparks flew. Tongues of flame began to spread into the passageway and the door frame of the potato room caught light. Down in their cellar smoke started to curl through the cracks between the floorboards and the children could hear a sullen roar as the fire grew in intensity.

'Oh dear, what have we done?' wailed Sarah.

Chapter Nine

ESCAPE

The first inkling the guards had of the fire was a cloud of thick black smoke billowing from the staircase that led to the courtyard. They immediately raised the alarm and other Urgils came running from all parts of the fortress. Gublak himself, accompanied by Crow, hurried to find out the cause of the commotion. As soon as he realized what was happening he barked a series of orders to his guards. His mind leapt to the obvious conclusion. The children had started the fire as a distraction in order to make good their escape. He was consumed with a cold fury that this should happen just as the Star-Pearl was within his grasp.

'The wretches will not get far,' he snarled. 'Ulris will see to that. And then they will pay dearly for this.'

He called forth the wolf pack and rapidly explained what had happened. At once the wolves, led by Ulris, shot from the fortress gates and began to snuffle about for the scent.

Meanwhile, the guards were doing the best they could to contain the fire. There was little water available in the fortress so they had no way of extinguishing it. Instead they used axes to hack away all the wood surrounding the exits to the kitchens in the hope of preventing the fire from spreading. It was difficult work, for the heat was intense and the smoke suffocating.

Suddenly an almighty crash was heard as the roof caved in. A fiery fountain of sparks cascaded over the toiling Urgils and threatened to set fire to the adjoining rooms. They had to use what water was available to douse the floors. This may have saved the children's lives, for some of the water flooded across the floor of the potato store and prevented it from igniting.

Grim-faced, Gublak watched the blaze from the courtyard above. He would show no mercy to those children when Ulris caught them!

But Ulris and his band, in spite of an extensive search, did not find them. The leader came panting back to his master.

'There is no scent or trail, your Eminence,' he growled. 'I do not believe they have left the castle.'

'Then they are hiding somewhere,' Gublak answered. 'Search the grounds and every room.'

Meanwhile he descended the stair to the corridor which led to the remains of the kitchens. The two guards who had been on kitchen duty were still fighting the blaze, though it was by now burning less fiercely. He demanded to know what had happened. In the darkness of their cellar the children listened with bated breath as the guards recounted the events leading up to the fire.

'They have sought to thwart my plans. Well, they shall not escape. I shall burn them alive when they are caught,' growled the goblin.

'Sir, is it not possible that they have all perished in the fire?' ventured Gurk.

The goblin spoke with an icy rasp. 'If they have

then you shall undergo the same fate.' The Urgils shuddered. 'But I do not think so. Even now the wolves and guards are searching every room. They will soon be found. As for you, go join them. Your punishment I will decide when they are caught.'

The children and the princess heard the sound of the soldiers' rapidly retreating footsteps followed by the slow tread of Gublak.

'I reckon it's now or never,' whispered Peter as soon as all was quiet.

'What about the wolves?' asked Sarah.

'You heard what he said. They're searching the castle. This is probably the only chance we're going to get,' said Andrew. 'We'd better take it.'

'Right, then, give me a moment to open the trapdoor,' said Peter.

He stumbled around until he found the sack of potatoes they had positioned underneath the trapdoor. Balancing himself precariously on it, he pushed up at the flap.

'It won't budge,' he gasped. 'It's stuck or something.'

'Here, let me help,' Andrew volunteered. He joined his brother on the sack but he was not tall enough to reach. Nor, for that matter, was Sarah.

'Oh dear, what are we going to do?' she cried.

'Alena, you're nearly as tall as Peter. You'd better give him a hand,' Andrew said.

The princess sat huddled in a corner, shivering. She did not answer.

'Alena, where are you?' Peter demanded.

'Over here,' she stuttered.

'What's the matter?'

'I'm scared.'

'Well, come on, pull yourself together and help me get this open.'

Sarah groped for the princess's hand in the dark and pulled her across to Peter. Somehow, between them they managed to get her on to the potato sack and Sarah and Andrew did their best to hold both steady.

'Now push,' gasped Peter. 'Come on, push hard.'

The trapdoor began to open under their combined efforts and the four of them were immediately sprayed with a dirty mixture of ash and water.

'Ugh,' cried Andrew. 'I've just got a faceful.'

'Well, you'll have to put up with it for the moment,' said Peter. 'Now I'll try to hold this open while you climb out, Alena. All right?'

He pressed up with all his might as she released her hold and tried to climb through the gap. She scrabbled for a grip while Peter gritted his teeth and bore the weight of the lid and, of course, the potato sack which still rested on top of it. His back and arms were agonizing, and sweat stood out on his brow. He couldn't last much longer. But neither had the princess the strength to haul herself out.

'I can't do it,' she gasped in fright. 'I'm slipping.'

'Put your feet on my shoulders,' said Sarah. 'Go on. I'll hold you.'

It worked, and somehow she managed to squeeze out. She was only just in time, for Peter's strength gave out and he collapsed on top of his brother and sister. Up above, Princess Alena heaved the sack off the lid and soon had it open. Moments later, all four stood in the smoke-blackened room. They were filthy.

'Well done, Alena,' said Peter. 'We'd never have got out without you.'

She gave him a watery smile. 'You'd never have been here in the first place if it were not for me,' she said.

'Never mind all that,' Andrew interrupted. 'We'd better get a move on. Everybody got their food sack? Come on, let's get out of here.'

The four crept stealthily along the corridor. They hardly dared breathe and expected to be caught at any moment. Up the short stair and they were able to spy out the land. The courtyard was empty and the side entrance through which they had lugged provisions was unguarded. Though only a few metres away, the open space between them and the gate seemed terribly exposed as they prepared to make a dash for it.

'You go first, Andrew, then Sarah. You after that, Alena, and I'll come last,' ordered Peter.

One by one, with a quick glance to the right and left, they darted across to the shelter of the archway.

'So far so good,' Peter panted. 'Now let's make for the coast as fast as we can. We'll have to go through the forest. No use going down the track. Let's just hope we don't meet any wolves.'

They began to descend the steep hillside and were soon deep in the undergrowth. Once under the cover of the trees they felt much safer and before long were scampering from tree to tree with ever-increasing confidence.

'That was a great plan, Peter,' yelled Andrew. 'Did you see the mess that fire made? Wonder the whole castle didn't burn down.'

'I wish it had,' he called back.

'Any idea how we're going to get off the island?'

'No, not yet. I just hope we can find a boat somewhere.'

'Do you think we've really got away with it?' puffed Sarah. 'It seems too good to be true.'

'Yes,' cried Andrew. 'They'll still be searching all over the castle. It'll take them ages yet. And in the end they'll probably think we've been burnt alive.'

But he had reckoned without Ulris.

The cunning wolf was not leader of the pack for nothing. He was intelligent and swift-witted as well as a ferocious fighter. Leaving others to search the furthest ends of the fortress, he padded back to the remains of the kitchen. And there he found what he was looking for. Footprints in the ashes. It took him but moments to work out how the children had foiled everyone. With a snarl he bounded up the stairs and leapt into the courtyard where he raised a blood-curdling howl of alarm.

Wolves came leaping down corridors and through doors in answer to his call. Gublak leaned from a window.

'What is it, Ulris?' he demanded.

'They have fooled us, Eminence. Hidden all the time in a cellar they were. They have fled while we looked elsewhere.'

'Then after them!' cried Gublak. 'But bring them back alive. I wish to supervise their deaths personally. Away now!'

The wolf pack tore through the gates at his command and were soon hot on the trail.

Far below, the children heard Ulris' alarm.

'They've found out,' Sarah cried. 'Now what'll we do?'

'Keep moving, faster,' said Peter grimly.

Princess Alena looked a picture of despair. Fear paralysed her legs and she sank to the ground.

'I can't go on,' she gasped.

'Don't be stupid,' Sarah screamed. 'Come on.'

She grabbed the princess's hand and yanked her to her feet so hard that she had to stumble on down the hillside.

'Faster,' urged Andrew. 'I can hear them.'

The howls of the wolves seemed to fill the air and terror lent wings to the children's feet. They fairly flew down the hillside.

Suddenly they broke from the trees into a broad clearing, and the ground fell away sharply before them into a steep ravine. By now they were going so fast that it was impossible to stop and one by one they slithered and rolled to the bottom. Scrambling to their feet they ran on blindly, heedless of their direction.

It took only a few moments for them to discover they were trapped. Straight ahead was a blank grey cliff wall. The children came to a standstill and looked wildly about them. On all sides the gully rose steeply. There was no way out.

'Now what do we do?' cried Princess Alena in dismay.

Before anyone could answer there was a crashing in the trees and the fearsome grey form of Ulris appeared above them. His yellow eyes glinted as he sighted them and his jaws slavered with anticipation.

'Ulris is not so easily fooled,' he grated. He motioned with his head and the pack spread out. They began to wind their way down the ravine towards where the children stood cowering in defeat.

Chapter Ten

THE WHIRLPOOL

'I told you to leave me behind,' Princess Alena blub-
bered. 'I didn't want to come with you in the first
place. Now look what has happened.'

'Oh, don't be ridiculous,' Sarah scolded. 'We're all
in this together, whether you like it or not.'

They stared helplessly as the hungry-looking
wolves drew ever closer.

'Oh, please, Elmesh, Oswain, someone help us,'
Sarah prayed silently.

'You sure we can't make a belt for it, Pete?'
Andrew muttered.

His brother shook his head. 'There's nowhere to
go, is there?' He glanced back at the cliff—and then
looked again in amazement. There, against the rocky
face, stood the old shepherd.

'Look, everybody,' he cried.

The others turned.

'We've been saved,' exclaimed Sarah. 'Come on,
he'll show us the way again.'

They ran to where the shepherd was. He didn't
speak but with the tip of his crook traced the outline
of a door upon the rock. A moment later he vanished
from their sight. But a faint blue line remained
shimmering on the cliff.

'It's a door of some kind,' said Peter and ran towards it.

He could see no way of opening it.

'Perhaps you have to say "Open, sesame",' Andrew suggested. He shouted, 'Abracadabra, open sesame,' at the top of his voice. Nothing happened.

'Don't be silly,' Sarah replied. 'It must be Elmesh's doing. This is *real* magic. Oh, if only we had Gilmere again.'

'But we have,' cried Peter with a flash of inspiration. 'Or near enough. What about your Star-Pearl, Alena? That could do it.'

'Oh, that!' she sniffed. 'All that's done is cause trouble. It won't do any good.'

'Get it out anyway,' Sarah urged.

'Well, all right. But we may as well give up, you know.'

She reached into her blouse and drew out the jewel. By now the wolves were little more than a hundred metres away and came steadily loping towards their prey.

Peter was urgent. 'Point it at the outline,' he said.

Princess Alena reluctantly did so, but nothing happened. Sarah was beside herself with exasperation.

'Oh, for goodness sake, Alena, *believe* in it, just for a moment. Come on, all of us.'

They concentrated hard and whether it was the threat of the wolves or something more, the princess did manage to believe in the Star-Pearl's power.

'Open in the name of Elmesh,' ordered Peter.

At once, a fiery blue beam blazed forth from the jewel and hit the faint outline of the door. It sparkled to life with an electric blue flame and before their wondering gaze a door swung open. There before them was a tunnel lit at the far end by a pale ghostly glow.

'Quick,' cried Peter. 'It's worked. Run for it!'

Ulris, who was at the head of the wolves and only fifty metres away, saw what had happened. With a snarl of fury he leapt forwards.

The children sprinted along the tunnel as swiftly as their legs could carry them, but the wolves were gaining. Faster and faster they ran. The howling and panting of their pursuers was magnified in the passage and they seemed almost at their heels. Hopes that the magic door would keep the wolves out were dashed.

The pale light ahead grew closer and they wondered if it was simply daylight at the other end—in which case all would be lost. But it proved to be more daunting still, for the tunnel came to an abrupt dead end.

To their amazement, they saw that the light came from a rapidly whirling pool of water fed by a small waterfall gushing from the roof. There was no way forwards and the wolves were almost upon them.

'We must have to jump in the pool,' gasped Andrew.

'It's no good,' screamed Princess Alena. 'We're trapped.'

'Get in,' snapped Peter. 'It's got to be right. Come on, it's our only hope. Hold your breath.'

He gave the princess a push and she fell with a cry into the glowing whirlpool, to be instantly swallowed up. Sarah and Andrew looked at each other for courage then plunged in together. Peter turned to find himself face to face with Ulris.

'There is no escape for you though, is there?' He bared his fangs and advanced. In sheer desperation Peter threw himself into a back-flip and dived into the whirlpool, thinking for a brief instant what a good job he had been practising that all summer.

Down and down he was sucked at dizzying speed. He tried opening his eyes for a moment and was dazzled by a kaleidoscope of rushing colours. His head span in the confusion of light and he lost consciousness.

Up above, a defeated Ulris growled with rage and watched as the light went out in the pool. Neither he nor any in his pack dared venture into the whirling black waters which remained.

.　　.　　*　　.　　.

Peter stirred slightly and smiled to himself. He gave a contented grunt and snuggled into a more comfortable position on the soft surface. He felt warm and relaxed and half-dreamed he was adrift on a sunlit sea.

It was Andrew's shout which made him open his eyes. He gave a small start of surprise, for he found himself lying on sand. He jerked upright and looked about him to find he was on a gently-shelving beach and waves were lightly lapping the shore. The splashing of water behind made him turn to see a stream pouring from the rocky cliff and soaking away into the sand. Not far away lay his sister and Princess Alena. Andrew was already sitting up.

'Hey, Pete, what's happened to us? Where are we?'

'Haven't a clue,' he replied. 'Last thing I remember was being sucked down that whirlpool.'

'Me too.'

Andrew staggered to his feet and stumbled across to his brother. 'Are the girls all right?' He gave his sister a shake. 'Sarah?'

'Mm,' she smiled and stretched. 'I feel so nice. Are

we in heaven or something?'

'No, I don't think so,' Peter replied seriously. 'On a beach somewhere. I think we somehow got washed down to the shore,' he explained, and showed them both the stream.

'Well, it's got to be that shepherd's doing,' declared Sarah. 'Somebody's on our side, at least.'

'Good job, too,' replied Peter with feeling. 'I didn't fancy our chances against those wolves.'

At this, Princess Alena flinched and sat bolt upright. 'W. . .where are we? Where are the wolves?' she asked with alarm.

The others laughed. 'It's all right, Alena,' said Peter gently. 'We're safe now—at least, for the moment.'

They studied their surroundings. The food sacks had been washed down with them and miraculously the food was dry. In fact, even their clothes showed no sign of being drenched. As far as anyone could see they were still on the island, for the mainland was recognizable across the straits. Nobody had any idea how long they had slept, but their stomachs told them lunch was overdue. So, before exploring further they drank from the stream and ate some food.

'You know, this is all very nice,' said Peter, 'but we really must get off this island. Somehow I don't think Gublak will have given up the search.'

'I agree,' Andrew said. 'For all we know they might be combing the island right now. They may even know about this stream.'

'Then what are we waiting for?' Sarah exclaimed in alarm. 'We must find a boat. It's too far to swim.'

They trotted down to the seashore in order to obtain a better view, but whichever part of the island they were on, it was completely deserted. The sand stretched monotonously in both directions until it curved away out of sight. Behind them, above the low cliffs, the forest rose dark and forbidding towards the summit. Somewhere just out of sight must be Gublak's fortress. The sky was clear blue and empty. There seemed nothing the children could do to make good their escape.

It was just then that Andrew spotted something. 'Hey, look. Out there.' He pointed across the sea.

For a moment nobody could see what he was indicating. Then they spied the graceful grey creatures leaping through the waves.

'Why, they're dolphins!' exclaimed Sarah. 'Look there are four of them.'

'No, five,' Peter corrected. 'See.'

'They're coming this way,' yelled Andrew excitedly, and to their wonder the beautiful creatures drew right into the shallows. One of them, by far the largest, rose out of the water on his tail, as dolphins do, and waved his flippers. The children laughed. Then he spoke. The voice was unlike anything they had ever heard. It was deep and strangely musical, and reminded Sarah afterwards of a cello.

'We have heard your song,' he said, or rather, hummed.

'What song?' Peter called, puzzled.

'Why, the music of the singing stone. Sweet it was, as the shimmering of the sea beneath a thousand stars. Fair, clear as moonbeams caressing a coral strand. It drove us into joy and we are come to serve its sound.'

'What's he talking about?' whispered Andrew to Peter.

'I'm not sure, but maybe he means Alena's jewel,' he replied.

As if in answer to the question, the dolphin spoke again. 'Which favoured one bears the stone? And

87

what service may we bring?'

'Go on, Alena,' Andrew urged. 'It must be you.'

The princess stepped forward hesitantly. 'I am Alena and I bear such a stone,' she said. 'We need to cross the sea to the mainland but we have, as you see, no means. If you could help us in some way we would be most grateful.'

The dolphin flipped beneath the waves and re-emerged with his companions only to repeat the action in a series of splendid dives.

'Our delight knows no bounds,' he sang at last. 'We shall bear you ourselves to the shore you seek. Come, sit upon our backs. And I, fair stone-bearer, would have you ride with me, if such privilege I may enjoy.'

And so the children waded out into the shallows and soon found themselves astride the backs of these magnificent animals. The journey was enthralling. The dolphins carved effortlessly through the waves. At times they leapt in graceful arcs and wove between one another in criss-crossing paths. The children, though soaked to the skin and covered in sea spray, would not have missed the experience for anything. They laughed and screamed with delight at the breathtaking antics of their hosts.

Throughout the journey each of the dolphins hummed a continuous note which not only seemed just right for the child he carried but was also in perfect harmony with that of his companions. The music made the children feel very safe.

The land they were approaching proved to be a rugged coastline rising at once to high mountains. Before long they came to the shallow waters of a small pebbly bay and drew to rest. They slipped from the shoulders of their sea-steeds and bade them thanks. The leader of the school looked with friendly eyes upon the four.

'Farewell, good speed, my friends. May Elmesh guide your steps upon this foreign land. Let his music keep your hearts from fear.'

With that the dolphins were off. The children waded to shore and waved wistful goodbyes as their friends cavorted northwards.

The sun was still high, so the first thing they did was to let their clothes dry in its heat. Most of their food was ruined except for some fruit and cheese, but nobody was too worried. To be free from the island and Gublak was sufficient. They lay back contentedly and chatted about the dolphins and what it felt like riding them.

All of a sudden Alena sat up. The others turned. She was looking pale.

'What's up, Alena?' Peter asked.

She pointed to the sky at a black speck in the distance.

'I have a feeling that's Crow,' she said.

They watched as the bird grew smaller. It was heading back to the island.

'Then this is no place for us to hang about,' said Peter firmly. 'Let's be on our way.'

Chapter Eleven

THE SLABS OF DRINGOL

The beach marked the bottom of a steep valley where a stream had slashed its wild way down the mountainside. All around towering cliffs dropped sheer into the sea. The only way inland was to climb the mountain by following the rugged course of the brook.

'At least we won't be short of water,' Andrew said cheerfully as they scrunched up the beach towards the grassy lower slopes of the valley.

Peter didn't reply. He looked serious. A little bit of mountain walking had taught him how dangerous it is to lead an unequipped party even in familiar territory, let alone across unknown terrain without map or compass. He was not even sure if this was the right way; it was just the only way. He tried not to let his feelings show.

'Come on, everyone,' he shouted. 'Let's keep together and get a move on. It's mid-afternoon already and we've a long way to go.'

A chorus of groans greeted him but they did as he said.

At first the journey was quite easy and they were able to tramp steadily up the valley to the cheerful chatter of the stream as it wound its way between the boulders. But their path began to rise and it was not long before everyone was puffing and blowing. The grass gave way to shattered rock and often they were having to use their hands to clamber over the larger boulders. In spite of this, they managed to keep going for about an hour before Peter called a proper halt.

'Phew, I feel done in,' exclaimed Sarah. 'I thought you were never going to stop.'

'Well, I wanted us to get a good start,' he explained. 'We'll not be able to go so fast from now on. You all right, Andrew?'

His brother smiled cheerfully from a bright red face.

'How about you, Alena?'

She smiled a brief acknowledgement but did not look at all happy. The others gave one another knowing glances.

'Well, let's have five minutes break, anyway,' Peter said brightly.

The view was stunning. The valley fell away in a broad sweep of jumbled brown and grey rocks. Sunlight glittered on the water as it cascaded over ledges and boulders. Far below through the haze they could see the little pebble beach looking now no bigger than a cornflake.

'Any idea how far we've climbed, Pete?' asked Andrew.

'Difficult to say but maybe two hundred and fifty metres,' he replied.

He shaded his eyes against the sun and stared into the distance. The sea was misty blue and the horizon lost in haze but he could make out the island and what looked like Gublak's fortress on top. He squinted to see more detail. A movement caught his eye. From around the northern tip of the island a dark shape was emerging. He kept silent and watched. Then it dawned on him. *Grimwolf* had set sail and was heading in their direction!

'On your feet, everybody,' he said quickly. 'They're after us.'

The others followed his gaze and needed no further encouragement to be on their way.

'I bet that's Crow's doing,' said Andrew with disgust.

In spite of feeling a bit stiff after their rest the desire to increase the distance between them and their pursuers urged them on. But the mountain was slowing them down. It was growing very steep and they were having to clamber most of the way. Peter hoped they would not reach a point where ropes would be necessary. Their only hope lay in sticking by this brook. He glanced across at Alena. She looked very glum. Something was up.

It was as they reached a difficult part that the crisis broke. Peter had just helped Sarah and Andrew over a slippery slab of rock and was waiting as the princess attempted it. Her foot slipped and she stumbled.

'It's no good,' she cried in exasperation. 'I can't go on. I want to go back.'

The children were dumbfounded.

'You what?' said Andrew incredulously when he found his voice.

'I want to go back. Do you hear?' she shouted at them.

'But they'll kill you,' said Andrew.

'Not while I have the Star-Pearl.'

'But he'll get it off you,' cried Sarah.

'Don't be a fool. He wants me to share it with him,' she responded angrily. Her voice sounded strange as though she were not quite herself.

'But don't you realize it's all a trick?' said Peter.

'I shall be a great princess,' she exclaimed imperiously. 'I shall have all I desire if I return.'

'But you're already a princess,' he insisted.

She sat down and tears came to her eyes. 'But that's the whole point. I'm not. Don't you see I have nothing to return to? I'm an orphan. If I go with you I shall only be pretending to be a princess. If I return to Gublak at least it will be my choice.'

'But surely being adopted into the royal family makes you a real princess?' Peter persisted.

By now Princess Alena was growing hysterical. 'Oh, stop going on,' she screamed. 'You don't understand. I hate being adopted. I hate this mountain. I hate everybody! Now get out of my way. I'm going down.'

She rose trembling to her feet and made to depart, but Peter restrained her. He knew that one of the most important things on mountains was not to lose your nerve. He had to take charge. For a long tense moment the princess and he stared at each other. It was a battle of wills. Then suddenly she relaxed and collapsed into a tearful heap.

'Oh, I'm sorry,' she sobbed. 'But . . . it's these voices in my head. They keep saying things to me. I've had it all the way up, ever since we left the beach, and I can't stand any more.'

'I knew something was wrong,' said Sarah.

'Why didn't you say so earlier?' Peter asked the princess.

'I don't know,' she wailed. 'I don't know anything any more. Oh, why don't you go on? Leave me behind. You'll be all right. It's me they want.'

'Look, let's not start that again,' Peter said in a matter-of-fact voice. 'Nobody is going back. We're here to rescue you and that's what we're going to do. So come on.'

Reluctantly she got to her feet.

'Right, now try that rock again.'

To her surprise the princess managed quite easily this time. She was beginning to respect Peter. To cheer her up, Sarah and Andrew sang their version of 'Ten green bottles' which was 'Ten green goblins standing on a ball'. She laughed and felt better.

Soon, however, their route became too steep for singing. In spite of the struggle, Peter allowed them only brief rests. It was no longer possible to see the beach and he wondered if the pirates had landed.

The sun was rapidly dropping and the air grew cool. Mist was gathering far out to sea and shadows beginning to fall. There was no wind and a heavy stillness hung in the air. The only sound was the chilly tinkle of the brook. Peter knew they could not go much further before needing to seek shelter for the night. Thankfully, the brow of the valley was just above them and it could be downhill after that.

When they reached the crest five minutes later it was just as though they had entered another world. Right before them, lying still and dark in the shadows thrown by the setting sun, was a calm mountain lake. This was the source of the stream they had been following. Rising from it on all sides but theirs were steep slabs of fissured rock which appeared quite impassable.

But most daunting of all was the breathtaking sweep of a snow-covered hanging valley which stretched away to the distant skyline and which had been out of sight from below.

Peter's heart sank. There was no way they could hope to climb further that day. In fact, he couldn't see how they would ever master the awesome slabs which lay ahead. It looked as though they were stuck—and the pirates could well be upon them by nightfall. Turning glumly to his companions he gave a shrug of despair. He felt like crying.

Just then, they heard a shout. Each one whirled about to see where it came from. Hearts thumped wildly. Surely the pirates weren't here already?

'Ho!' cried the voice again.

Striding with such ease across the slabs that you would be forgiven for thinking they were flat ground came a short, thickset human-like figure. He wore a sheepskin jerkin and leather breeches and was armed with a staff and a fearsome axe. A long sheathed knife hung from his broad belt.

'Why, it's a dwarf,' whispered Sarah.

He drew near and stood, legs astride, before them.

'And what are you strangers about, trespassing upon my domain?' he demanded. His voice was deep and gruff. He didn't look at all friendly.

'Please, sir, we didn't know we were on anybody's private property,' Peter replied politely. 'We landed on the beach below and are travelling across the mountain to the land beyond.'

The dwarf eyed him suspiciously. 'Why should you wish to come this way?' he questioned sharply.

'It seemed to be the only way,' the boy replied. He didn't feel it wise to reveal too much to this stranger. 'Actually, we're a bit lost. So, if you'll kindly show us the way we'll leave your land as soon as possible.'

'You are by the Slabs of Dringol,' the dwarf replied. 'I am Dringol and this is my domain. None pass but by my permission, and that I give to few. Why should I grant you passage?'

Peter was at a loss for words. Sarah stepped forwards. 'Please, sir, we don't wish to intrude but nor do we want to go all the way back to the beach. Have pity on us travellers and let us through.'

The dwarf looked with interest at Sarah's blonde

hair and then at the golden head of Princess Alena. His thick lips parted in a sort of smile.

'Very well. I shall grant your request. But it shall not be for nothing. With what shall you pay me for my pains?' His eyes gleamed. 'Gold I like, and silver and jewels. Do you have any?'

The children shook their heads. Then Princess Alena thought of her Star-Pearl and was about to say something when Andrew caught her out of the corner of his eye. He gave her a sharp but sly kick in the ankle which made her cry out in pain.

'Sorry, I must have kicked something,' Andrew said. He bent down to where she was rubbing her ankle and whispered through the side of his mouth, 'Keep quiet about it. Say nothing.'

The dwarf eyed them inquisitively.

'Are you sure you have no jewels for me?'

'The only thing we can offer is what food we have in our sacks,' said Peter with dignity.

The dwarf looked disappointed and hesitated a few moments. Peter did not trust his cunning eyes. 'Very well. I shall take all you have as the price of a path.'

One by one they handed over their sacks. He flung them across his shoulders and then stomped off, leaving the children to follow. After skirting the lake for a while, he suddenly came to a halt. The children wondered what he was about to do. He turned to them.

'You cannot traverse the Slabs of Dringol but there is a path beneath the mountain which leads to the ridge. I shall take you that way.'

With that he tapped his staff against a rock. Immediately it rolled back to reveal a dimly lit tunnel. He strode in. The children hesitated.

'I do not wait for strangers,' he said. 'Come now.'

With much misgiving they entered the mouth of the tunnel. At once the rock rumbled back into place, shutting out the daylight with a resounding crash. It felt as if the mountain had swallowed them. The dwarf gave a hollow laugh which echoed and boomed along the subterranean corridors.

Chapter Twelve

ŔIDDLES

The tunnel was lit by a flaming torch which Dringol removed from a bracket on the wall. It made shadows dance on the rough-hewn rock. The four children waited in trepidation as the dwarf's laughter echoed in the silence.

'Why are you afraid?' he boomed. 'I mean you no harm. Have we not struck a bargain, eh? I shall fulfil the price of what you have paid me. Come, follow me.'

The children, with no choice but to trust their host, began to file after him. The tunnel was not very high and Peter had to stoop most of the way, which made it a very uncomfortable journey for him. Their path twisted and turned but all the while rose steadily. Every so often they would pass the blank black holes of other tunnels leading off to the right or left. Where or to what they led, none could guess. They trembled with the knowledge that they were completely at the dwarf's mercy.

Soon they were perspiring freely, for it was very warm under the mountain and Dringol was moving fast.

At length the path dipped slightly and they entered a lofty cavern from which several tunnels led off in different directions. Here the dwarf stopped.

He turned to the children and gave them a shrewd look from beneath beetled brows.

'Many are the ways beneath the mountain and Dringol knows them all. But what if I should leave you now? Would you not be lost for ever—doomed to wander the nameless deeps of the earth till the end of time?'

The children said nothing. Then Peter spoke solemnly. 'You gave us your word you would lead us to the top of the ridge.'

'Ah, my word. Yes, my word. As truly as you gave me yours, indeed. All you had to give was your food, eh?'

Peter felt uncomfortable under his piercing gaze. The dwarf continued, 'Let us play a little game before we proceed. Do you like games? I will ask a riddle or two. And if you guess the answer correctly I will lead you further, but if not. . . .'

'But that's not fair,' interrupted Sarah.

'Hang on a moment,' said Andrew. He laid a restraining hand on his sister's arm. 'I think that's a smashing idea, Mr Dringol. Only let's make it more interesting. We'll ask a riddle as well, and, as you are older and wiser, we only have to answer yours if you can answer ours. And if you can't answer ours you must lead us on.'

The dwarf looked irritated and Andrew wondered if he would take up the challenge.

'Oh, very well,' he snapped. 'But I ask mine first.'

Andrew agreed. The dwarf peered at each of them in turn before speaking.

'From whom fly four
To Dringol's lair;
Green, fat and rich
Midst sea so fair?'

99

The children glanced uneasily at each other. They knew the answer and began to guess the dwarf's cunning purpose. Dringol smirked. But Andrew was not to be outdone.

'Well, here's mine,' he said. 'What's the difference between a wet day and a lion with toothache?'

Dringol frowned and muttered to himself. The children waited anxiously as he strode round and round in small rapid circles. At length he stopped.

'I give up,' he said angrily.

'Then we don't have to guess the answer to yours,' said Peter. 'Now you must keep your bargain and lead us to the ridge.'

Dringol growled to himself but reluctantly agreed. They set off through one of the tunnels, the children almost running in order to keep up with him.

'Well done, Andrew,' Sarah puffed. 'Where did you get that one?'

'Christmas cracker,' he replied with a grin. 'Do you know the answer?'

'I think so,' she answered. 'Um, one is pouring with rain and the other is roaring with pain.'

He nodded.

On and on they hastened until the children lost all track of how long they had been under the mountain. There was nothing else to do but keep up with the flickering torch as it wound its way ever upwards along this endless corridor.

Seemingly ages later, they came to another cave in which a small fire burned. Dringol called a halt and promptly sat down. The others gratefully did the same. He opened the four sacks and spilled out the remains of the food on the ground.

'Hm, not a generous gift for such a journey,' he said as he eyed the few apples, pears and bits of cheese. 'But it will do . . . for the moment.'

The children and the princess were obliged to sit and watch as the dwarf greedily devoured all the food. Not once did he offer them a bite. It made them realize how hungry they were and Peter wondered how they would survive the journey down the mountain without food.

Dringol licked his lips and eyed the children. 'Time for the next game of riddles, I think.'

Peter, Sarah and Princess Alena glanced at Andrew and hoped he had a good one ready. The dwarf recited:

> 'Sails on the sea
> With jaws stained red,
> Who can this be
> The travellers dread?'

Sarah looked at Peter with dismay. The dwarf knew too much. If they had to answer this one he would surely demand to know why they were running away. Then the game would be up. He would soon be after the Star-Pearl. Andrew spoke up.

> 'A hiss, a bellow and a "gloop",
> Four lines on yellow, then they stop.
> What is it?'

The dwarf sank his head on to his chest as folk do when they are thinking. He muttered Andrew's riddle over and over again to himself. Even Peter, Sarah and the princess looked puzzled. Andrew just smiled.

At last, the dwarf leapt to his feet and glowered at him. 'I don't know,' he growled.

'Then lead us on, please, as we agreed,' Peter said quietly, though he felt afraid.

'Very well,' he snapped. 'But be warned, you shall

not get the better of me again.'

And with that he stomped off, leaving them to follow.

'Phew, well done, Andrew,' whispered Peter. 'But what was the answer? I couldn't work it out.'

Andrew chuckled. 'Oh, it's easy. It's an elephant skating on a bowl of cold custard!'

Some while after, they began to climb a long spacious stair. Up and up it went as far as the flickering torch would light it. The children plodded wearily after the tireless dwarf. They were ready to drop by the time they reached the top. Dringol halted. To their dismay they saw by the light of his torch no more than a short upward-sloping tunnel which led to a dead end.

Peter gathered himself to protest when the dwarf pointed his staff. To their immense relief a stone rolled back to reveal a starlit sky and the cold snow shining beneath its light. Chill air blew upon them but it did not matter. Anything to be out of this hateful mountain and away from the wily dwarf.

'Thank you for leading us,' said Peter. 'If you just show us which is the path we'll be on our way.'

The dwarf suddenly barred their way with his staff. His lip curled in an evil leer.

'Not so fast, if you please. I do not feel satisfied for my labours. Nor do I believe you have told me all you should. So I have one more riddle for you. And this time you shall answer first. If you are wrong or cannot answer, I shall keep the golden haired ones.' He pointed to the girls. 'If you guess correctly . . . then we shall speak of what you might pay me for the last part of this journey. Now here is my riddle.

'Where meets the starlight
And the stone?

Who bears the birthright
To her throne?'

Peter knew the game was up. Whatever answer they gave would betray Princess Alena. Without a moment's thought he rushed at the dwarf as hard as he could and threw him off balance.

'Quick, run for it. Run for your lives!' he cried.

The others needed no second bidding. Andrew sprinted after his brother followed closely by Sarah and Princess Alena while the dwarf bellowed with rage behind them. Peter darted into the open air and immediately slithered on the snow. He grasped frantically at an exposed rock and clung on for dear life. The cave came out halfway down a steep icy slope which ended in a precipice.

Inside the tunnel Dringol recovered himself with a howl of fury, while the others ran towards the exit. The dwarf, however, pointed his staff ahead of them and muttered a deep spell. The rock began to close. Desperately, Andrew dived through the narrowing gap to freedom. But Sarah was not so fortunate. She stumbled so that both she and the princess were too late. With a cry of despair she fell against the fast shut rock.

Andrew was in even greater trouble. He landed on his front and before he could collect his wits began to slide spreadeagled down the slope. Peter watched horrified as he saw his brother slithering towards the edge of the precipice.

'Dig your feet in, Andrew,' he shrieked.

With agonizing slowness Andrew came to a halt and lay helplessly splayed out on the frozen snow, only metres from the drop.

'Pete, I'm stuck,' he gasped. 'What are we going to do?'

Peter looked frantically around him. How could he reach his brother? He couldn't even move safely himself. If only he had a rope or something. The cold began to bite into his body. His teeth chattered and panic welled up in his heart.

'Pete. Pete, I'm slipping again,' Andrew cried in terror. 'I can't stop myself.'

Chapter Thirteen

THE ICE MAIDEN

Peter looked around him for help and it was only as he realized there was none that he looked up to the heavens. And there he saw the bright star, El-la. An involuntary cry came to his lips.

'*Eko Elmesh e kala yento coella.*'

For a long moment nothing happened. Andrew continued to slide slowly to the brink of doom. Then something began to shimmer to Peter's left. A pillar of ice to which he had given no attention was glowing from within. Brighter and brighter the light grew until his eyes could bear it no more and he was forced to turn his head aside.

When he dared look again, to his amazement, there stood in the place of the pillar a lady—tall, pale and fair. Yet she was not cold; from where he clung so desperately to the rock Peter felt a warmth which cheered his heart. She smiled upon him.

He pointed to his brother. With a nod of understanding she gestured with her hand and he came to an immediate halt. Then, without a care, she strode with ease across that impossible icy slope to where Andrew lay helpless. Her long white robe flowed gracefully as she went.

She took him by the hand and helped him to his

feet. To his astonishment, Andrew found he could stand and walk without difficulty while holding her arm. Peter looked on with a mixture of joy, wonder and relief as they came towards him.

'Thank you. Oh, thank you so much,' he cried.

Without a word she took his hand and led both up the slope till they were on level ground and could stand unaided. Peter and Andrew felt overawed by her presence and hardly knew what to say.

'Thank you for rescuing me,' said Andrew.

'Who are you?' Peter asked.

'I am the Ice Maiden,' she replied. Her voice was soft and sweet. 'I came in answer to your cry.'

'I didn't know what I said,' Peter stammered.

'Sounded like a foreign language to me,' Andrew said.

The Ice Maiden smiled, 'It was not foreign to my ears, that is sufficient.' Her eyes sparkled with the starlight. 'Now what brings you to such a plight.'

'The girls!' gasped Peter. 'They never escaped in time. That evil dwarf has got them.'

Words tumbling from their lips, they told her all that had happened to them since they had met Dringol. The Ice Maiden listened patiently.

'The mountains are harsh and their laws stern.' She spoke gravely. 'Pray your companions have the heart to resist this dwarf.'

'Sarah will be all right,' said Andrew. 'It's Alena I'm worried about.'

'Then aid I will give to break the spell. But it will take a little time. Wish them well while I divine the way.'

.   .   *   .   .

In the dimly lit tunnel the girls shrank back against the wall as Dringol slowly advanced. He gave a booming laugh.

'Ah, foolish ones! It has worked better than I planned, for it is one of you two who has what I desire.'

'Don't you dare come any nearer,' Sarah screamed. 'You horrible, hateful beast!'

'And how shall you stop me?' he taunted.

He stood and folded his arms little more than two metres from where they cringed.

'It's all right, Sarah,' whispered Alena. 'He cannot take it from me by force. I'll be safe.'

'That doesn't help me much, does it?' Sarah replied sharply.

'Let me have the Star-Pearl and then you shall go free,' the dwarf demanded.

Slowly Princess Alena removed it from her blouse. The dwarf took a step forward.

'Stay where you are,' she ordered. 'I will not let you come closer.'

The Star-Pearl began to glow.

Dringol laughed but the moment he tried to take another step he found he could not. An invisible barrier had fallen between him and the girls. He pushed and shoved, then angrily muttered spells, but all to no avail.

'Well done,' cried Sarah. 'It's working.'

Princess Alena looked rather pleased with herself and giggled as the dwarf raged and fumed helplessly before them.

It was some time before his fury subsided and then a cunning gleam came into his eye. He sat down cross-legged and gazed at them.

'Well, well, now you are in a fine pickle,' he said. 'I cannot reach you and you cannot reach your companions. Between us we have made a neat prison for you, have we not? All I need to do is wait. Hunger and thirst will break your will. So, when you are ready, place the jewel on the floor before you.'

The girls turned to one another in dismay. Actually they were very hungry and especially thirsty. Just thinking about it made things worse. Dringol knew this and with a smirk on his face took a long swig from a flask which he carried in his belt.

For perhaps ten minutes nothing more happened. Dringol remained sitting on the floor and the two girls stood with their backs to the sealed rock. No one spoke and a thick silence hung over the tunnel. Until, suddenly, the dwarf cocked his head to one side.

'Ah, I hear something. The sound of others coming from afar. But not so very distant, I judge.' He regarded the girls with a mocking stare. 'We have visitors. I think you may be acquainted with them, eh?'

Sarah and the princess said nothing but both realized it must be their pursuers. To remain trapped like this would be disastrous. Gublak might well possess powers to break the spell of the Star-Pearl. And he would show no mercy, least of all towards Sarah. What should they do?

Dringol guessed what was going on in their minds.

'Give me the jewel and you may go free,' he said. 'You still have time to escape. If not, I shall lead your hunters to their quarry.'

Princess Alena began to sob. 'We cannot escape either way now. We will be lost. I told you I shouldn't have come with you.'

'Don't give up,' said Sarah. 'We're not finished yet.'

But the princess had been through enough. The voices jabbered in her head and she began to tremble uncontrollably. Her eyes became wild and staring.

She shrunk from Sarah and bared her teeth. Her voice changed as she spoke, one moment harsh and demanding, the next weak and pleading.

'I am Princess Alena. I will rule with Gublak. Fetch him to me . . . No, don't please. I'm afraid. I'm not a princess . . . an orphan, nobody . . . Don't touch me. I can destroy you. Bring me gold. I desire wealth. . . . No, I want to go home. I feel trapped, so helpless. . . . Gublak is my friend, my hope . . . No, he's a liar . . .'

Sarah was aghast as she watched the princess go to pieces. She didn't know what to do. When she tried to reach out her arms in comfort the princess merely knocked them away. The Star-Pearl began to fade. Dringol rubbed his stubby hands together with anticipation.

'Aha, now I have you,' he gloated. 'Give it to me.'

'Y. . .yes, t. . .take it,' said the princess through chattering teeth. 'It's of no use.'

'No, Alena, don't!' cried Sarah.

But the princess reached behind her neck to release the clasp. Dringol's eyes gleamed.

At that moment there was a deep rumble and the ground trembled beneath their feet. Then the rock which blocked off the tunnel began to crumble. All three shrank back, wondering what was going on. The next instant a blistering white light dazzled their eyes. Dringol screeched in terror and fled for his life. The two girls cowered on the ground, dreading to look.

The noise and light slowly faded until all was still. They waited apprehensively. Then to their surprise and delight they heard Peter's voice.

'Sarah, Alena. It's all right. You're safe!'

The two boys rushed in and flung their arms about the girls. The Ice Maiden stood smiling at the tunnel entrance as the children whooped and danced with delight.

'Thank goodness you came,' Sarah gasped. 'You were only just in time, you know. But how did you do it?'

Andrew grinned from ear to ear. 'We didn't,' he said. 'She did.'

For the first time Sarah and the princess noticed the Ice Maiden. Holding hands they slowly approached her graceful figure.

'Whoever you are, thank you.' There was awe in Sarah's voice as she spoke. 'I wondered if there was any hope for us.'

'Things are only hopeless when there is no hope in the heart,' she said. 'Now, you must be Sarah. And you are Princess Alena.'

'She's the Ice Maiden,' said Andrew. 'She saved my life.'

Between them Peter and his brother explained what had happened after their escape from the cave. How the Ice Maiden had appeared and rescued them. After leading them to a level place she had stood quietly singing to the stars before returning to the dwarf's door. Then her whole being began to pulsate with light until the boys had to shield their eyes—and the rock crumbled.

Sarah told the three of them what had taken place in the tunnel.

The Ice Maiden looked upon Princess Alena and spoke with understanding in her voice. 'Poor child,' she said to the still trembling girl. 'We must see what can be done.' She beckoned the others. 'Come now and do not fear. Dringol will not dare return as yet.'

'What about Gublak and his wolves?' Peter asked.

She laughed. 'They have a difficult journey to reach here. And though doubtless some shall pass they shall pay dearly for their trouble.'

Together they stood at the entrance and looked out on the snowy mountain and the awesome slope which had so nearly claimed Andrew's life.

'I cannot walk on that,' wailed the princess.

'Nor can I,' muttered Sarah.

'Don't worry. It's quite safe. You watch,' Andrew reassured them.

A pink glow seemed to radiate from the Ice Maiden and in its aura the children felt warm and secure. The girls found to their astonishment that they could walk quite easily on the treacherous ice.

The Ice Maiden led them up the slope until they came to a cave carved into solid blue-green ice. They were bidden to enter. The sight which met their eyes was magical. Before them lay a huge cavern of brightly lit ice. All the colours of the rainbow flashed and flickered about the crystalline walls. Great silvery icicles hung from the roof. Many-faceted shapes covered the floor in dazzling splendour.

'Wow!' cried Andrew. 'Is this where you live?'

The Ice Maiden nodded, evidently pleased at their reaction. She guided them down a broad crystal stair until they came to a small pool which lay green and still in the floor.

'This shall sustain and refresh you,' she explained and took four crystal goblets which she filled from the pool.

The liquid was warm and sweet, and the moment they tasted it a thrill ran through their bodies. It was as she had said and after one gobletful each felt as though they had eaten a three-course meal. Moments later drowsiness overtook them. Peter looked alarmed but the Ice Maiden laid a hand on his arm.

'Do not fear, Peter,' she whispered. 'You will rest only a short time before you resume your journey.'

She was so reassuring that he relaxed and was soon fast asleep. Andrew and Sarah likewise dozed off. Princess Alena made to lie down but the Ice Maiden restrained her.

'No, not you, Alena,' she said gently. 'Come with me, for we must speak and I would aid you.'

Together they walked back to the entrance and stood facing the stars. At the Ice Maiden's bidding Princess Alena told all her adventures. When she had finished the lady turned to her with a solemn look and then calmly cupped the Star-Pearl in her hand. The princess drew back in sudden panic, fearful lest the Ice Maiden should be harmed or should snatch it from her.

'Do not worry, child,' she reassured her. 'It will not harm me, nor would I steal it, for it is yours alone. But you have yet to realize the value of what you possess. Guard it well, for what you have treated as a trinket is so powerful it could change an empire. Many are they who would obtain it for that reason alone. Dark forces desire to wrest it from your grasp. Gublak has sought to seduce you into surrendering it. His greed is insatiable but serves purposes even more evil. You must understand this.'

'But what does it matter?' cried the princess. 'I am only an adopted child. How can this be called my birthstone. It's a lie.'

The Ice Maiden released the jewel.

'Adopted you are indeed, yet to those who receive a gift such as this it is as though they had been born into the royal line from the first. Unnamed you were, but Star-born you became. This is truly your birth-stone, Alena.' She emphasized the girl's name. 'Alena —if you relinquish it through carelessness, greed or folly, all will be lost. You become as nobody, and kingdoms fall. You yourself would grow corrupt beyond your imaginings. Can you see what is at stake?'

Princess Alena nodded quietly. 'I understand only a little of what you say, but I do see that I have been very foolish and brought myself and my companions to great danger. What shall I do? I do not know my own mind any longer. Can you help me?' She gazed up at the Ice Maiden with pleading eyes.

'You and your friends must complete the journey,' she replied. 'I see your healing lies at its end. Yet I may bring you comfort in your trial and a great measure of relief. See the star, El-la? Gaze upon it and hold the Star-Pearl in your grasp. I will sing for you.'

Princess Alena did as she was bidden and the Ice Maiden started to sing. The song was like nothing the princess had ever heard before.

It began with a soothing hum which gently rose and fell like the sighing of the wind in the trees. It took the princess in far-off memory back to when she lay in her mother's arms and heard her sing a lullaby.

The song broke into the merry chatter of birds as they greet the dawn. Laughter filled the princess's heart. She remembered her playmates. The Star-Pearl felt warm.

The Ice Maiden threw back her head and a triumphant melody resounded through the crags and valleys. It bore the strength of the rising sun as it conquers the remains of night and blazes over the horizon. The Star-Pearl burned hot in the princess's grasp and she loved her father.

Then the melody died away to be replaced by a high, silvery song of crystal clarity. Princess Alena knew she was hearing the long lost echoes of the music of the stars at the dawn of time. It was strange, magical and unearthly. She stood mesmerized. Tears rolled down her cheeks. In the back of her mind she heard the chatter of those mad voices but the sound was receding like a noisy crowd passing into the distance. Her head felt clear.

How long the song lasted or when it ended she could not say. It was only when the Ice Maiden spoke that she became aware of her surroundings.

'Come, Alena. It is done. Now we must wake your friends, for this night fast passes.'

The princess smiled and lovingly replaced the Star-Pearl within her blouse. 'Thank you,' she said simply.

It did not take long to rouse the others, who felt as if they had slept for days. The princess too felt refreshed but neither she nor the Ice Maiden spoke of what had happened.

So, accompanied by the Ice Maiden, they left the cave. With unerring steps she led them across the ridge and they began their descent on the other side just as the first pale hint of dawn was tingeing the eastern sky.

Before long, they could see their way. The pass down which they travelled ran right to the valley floor and soon they reached the line where the snow gave way to heather. Here the Ice Maiden stopped.

'Now I must leave you,' she explained. 'Elmesh go with you and give you courage.'

'Thank you ever so much for helping us,' said Peter. 'We would never have made it without you.'

'Oh, but we don't even know your name,' exclaimed Sarah.

For a brief instant the fair brow of the Ice Maiden clouded. 'Alas, it is decreed; my name I cannot tell but to him I shall one day love. Nor can I go further until that time shall come—whenever it may be,' she sighed.

There was an awkward silence which Andrew broke with his customary cheerfulness. 'Oh, well, I'm sure it'll come soon,' he said. 'Then you can tell us all about it.'

She smiled. 'One last thing. You have yet far to go and perhaps dangers to face. This will aid you should you need it.' She drew from her robe a large crystal and passed it to Peter. 'It will not melt while your heart is strong. Carry it well for it is destined to accomplish much more than your protection alone.'

Peter thanked her and placed it in his pocket.

'Farewell,' she cried and the next instant vanished from their sight.

The four companions turned towards the rising sun and began their descent into the green valley.

FLIP-FLOP

It was a happy party which wended its way down the
mountainside. All four chattered unceasingly about
their exciting adventures.

'I really thought I was a goner,' said Andrew.

'*You* did? You should have been in the tunnel with
us,' Sarah retorted. 'It was scary! Especially when we
thought Gublak was coming.'

She said nothing about Princess Alena's panic but
the princess spoke up for herself. 'I am sorry for
what happened then, Sarah. It was simply too much
for me.'

'Oh, that's all right,' she replied. 'It's over now.'

'Are you feeling better?' Peter asked the princess.

'Oh, much,' she answered. 'The Ice Maiden helped
me when you were asleep.'

Everyone thought the Ice Maiden was marvellous
and hoped they would meet her again sometime.
Sarah had ideas of her own.

The air grew warmer as they descended and it
promised to be a sunny day. A fine haze hung over
the land stretched out before them. It felt good to be
alive and for the moment they forgot all about their
enemies.

Which was why, perhaps, they did not notice the

'I wish I knew where we were going,' Peter muttered.

The party had reached the lowlands and ahead of them stretched a mixture of open woodland and grassy moors. From the sun's position they knew which way was east, but that was about all.

'Do you know where we are, Alena?' Andrew asked.

She shook her head. 'Not really. My home city must lie far to the north across the mountains. And somewhere this side must be the Great Forest. . . .'

'The Great Forest! Then that's where we must make for,' Sarah cried excitedly. 'Oswain will be there. And he's bound to help us.'

Princess Alena looked dubious. She felt uncomfortable every time she thought about her stepbrother. Sarah noticed this.

'Look, I know how you feel, Alena, but you've got to meet him. He's smashing, really he is. Anyway, I've had enough of crossing mountains for the moment.'

The others agreed that they must aim for the Great Forest, though nobody really knew what direction to take.

Just then they heard a strange noise coming from behind some bushes. It sounded something like, 'Nnnnughh! Phew!' They stopped and listened to this odd grunting, which was repeated several times over. Very cautiously all four crept closer and peered through the undergrowth. The most unexpected sight met their eyes.

A large brown rabbit dressed in a blue top coat with a yellow waistcoat and sporting a red spotted bow-tie was busily heaving something out of the ground. For a moment they wondered what on earth he was up to. Then out popped a large juicy carrot. He mopped his brow with a handkerchief which matched his bow-tie.

Sarah tried to stifle a giggle. The rabbit pricked up his ears at the sound and they thought he would bolt but instead he scratched his head and waddled in their direction. Peter went on his guard but he need not have worried.

'Oh, there you are,' exclaimed the rabbit as he rounded the bushes to where they crouched. 'I wondered where I might find you. Flip-flop's the name. Pleased to meet you.'

He held out a paw which Peter shook awkwardly. 'Pleased to meet you, too,' he mumbled. The others did the same.

'Who are you?' Princess Alena demanded.

'I told you, Flip-flop. I've been sent to look for you and lead you to Oswain.'

'You weren't doing much looking just then, were you?' said Andrew.

'Breakfast,' he replied. 'You know, the most delicious carrots grow in this part of the world. Best I've tasted since, oh, I don't know when.'

'We might have missed you altogether,' said Peter. 'Then what?'

'But you didn't,' the rabbit replied airily. 'Now how about breakfast? I for one am very hungry. Carrots, anyone?'

'He's nuts!' whispered Andrew.

The others agreed.

Still, carrots are better than nothing and they joined Flip-flop in devouring the pile he had pulled up. Sarah had a fit of giggles as she listened to all the crunching sounds and stared at this ridiculous rabbit.

'Are you sure it was Oswain who sent you?' Peter queried. The rabbit did seem the most unlikely guide imaginable. But then he recalled Fumble, Mumble and Grumble. They hardly gave you confidence at first sight.

'Oh, yes,' munched the rabbit. 'Though I must be honest and say I haven't done a lot of this sort of thing before. I volunteered, you know. Love travelling. Seeing the sights and all that.'

'Well, how far is it to Oswain?' demanded Andrew.

'How long is a healthy carrot?' Flip-flop returned. 'It depends if we stick to the main path or take the pretty route. I rather fancy the pretty one myself.'

'You do realize we're being followed, don't you?' said Princess Alena.

He raised a reassuring paw. 'Don't worry your head, Princess. Too much worry is bad for the digestion. You'll be quite safe with me. Have another carrot.'

Delighted as they were to have someone who would lead them to Oswain, the children wondered what they were letting themselves in for. They soon discovered the reason for his name, too. The rabbit had simply enormous flat feet which made a flip-flopping sound as he waddled along with his white tail bobbing from side to side. The children found it difficult not to laugh.

They followed a path of sorts but every so often Flip-flop would dart off to the left or right. At first the children thought he had spotted danger and kept diving for cover in the undergrowth. But each time he came back with either a lettuce or wild cabbage or another carrot. If that was not the reason, it was, as he explained to them, because he had seen 'something interesting'.

'This is getting ridiculous,' Peter declared. On this occasion they had left the obvious route and were stumbling through brambles and tussocks of long grass. 'Hey, Flip-flop, can't we keep to the path?'

'What's that?' cried the rabbit. 'This is much more

fun. Don't like paths much. Where's your sense of adventure?'

'I think I've had quite enough adventure for the moment,' Peter muttered as he unhooked himself from yet another bramble.

The next instant they heard an 'Oo! Ouch! Ah!' and Flip-flop vanished from their sight. They looked around in vain until a groan told them where he was. All four stumbled across to find the rabbit lying on the ground with his paws waving in the air.

'Ah, there you are,' he gasped. 'Help me up, will you?'

'What happened? Are you all right?' Andrew asked.

'Oh yes, silly me. I tripped over a rabbit hole,' he replied.

'How on earth can a rabbit trip over a rabbit hole?' Sarah exclaimed.

'Oh, I do it all the time,' he explained. 'Someone always leaves them in the wrong place.'

'That will teach you to keep to the path,' said Princess Alena. But, of course, it didn't.

They spent the whole day like this, stopping every so often to eat yet more vegetables which Flip-flop found, or to pick him up from another fall. If they were not doing that, it was pulling him out of the mud or trying to find the path after he had lost it.

On one occasion they found him stuck upside down in a hole with only his hind legs waving in the air because he had overbalanced and fallen in head-first while shouting 'Hallo'. They nearly split their sides laughing before they pulled him out.

Evening drew on and they all began to tire.

'Phew, can we stop soon?' Peter asked.

'Not yet,' Flip-flop replied. 'Not here.'

'Why not?'

'No breakfast.'

'Blow breakfast,' Andrew retorted. 'My legs ache. I want to rest.'

The rabbit halted.

'Tell you what. I know a short cut to breakfast from here.'

'Oh, no, not again!' they chorused.

'What do you mean "breakfast"?' Sarah asked.

'Carrots, of course. It's no use waking up without carrots, is it? Anyway, I like sleeping in a carrot bed.'

The others groaned.

'You and your stomach!' said Andrew.

However, in spite of their tiredness and misgivings the children agreed to take the short cut to where the carrots grew. It was one of the worst decisions they ever could have made. Especially as Crow spied their path from high above.

.　.　*　.　.

Later that evening, not so very far to the south-west, Gublak and Ulris met and made camp in an eerie stone hollow. The news from Crow was received with the greatest interest.

Chapter Fifteen

THE EARTH-TROG

Squelch!

Peter groaned as yet again his boot sank in the mud.

'Hey, Flip-flop, this ground's terribly boggy, you know.'

'Forgot to tell you that,' the rabbit replied. 'It's all right if you keep to the dry bits, though.'

'That's if we can find any dry bits,' Andrew called.

'I hope this is not too far,' said Princess Alena. 'The sun is beginning to set.'

'Hm, and it looks as though it might turn foggy,' Sarah added. 'I just hope that daft rabbit knows where he's going, that's all.'

It was fairly easy for Flip-flop to walk on this soggy ground because of his big feet. The others found it much more difficult so he had to keep waiting while they caught him up. He hadn't thought of this and the short cut was taking far longer than he'd planned.

As the sun set behind them it cast long shadows over the uneven ground. The air grew cool and misty. Ahead loomed the dusky phantoms of old gnarled trees. It was becoming very wet underfoot.

'I don't like the look of this,' Peter mumbled. 'Hey,

wait a bit, Flip-flop. Don't go so fast.'

'I can't see him,' said Sarah. 'I think we've lost him among those trees.'

The next instant, Peter put a foot wrong and his left leg sank so far into the bog that water poured over the top of his boot. The others had to pull him out.

'Yeuk! I'm soaked,' he complained. 'I've got a boot full of water. Go and find Flip-flop, will you, while I empty this out. And tell him to wait.'

The other three continued into the mist calling for Flip-flop as they went. Peter took off his boot and drained it. The fog closed in around him and by the time he had his boot back on again it was difficult to see where he was. The gloom was gathering and all the shadowy trees looked the same. Suddenly he felt afraid.

.　　.　　*　　.　　.

The stone hollow where Gublak and Ulris encamped was a place of ancient evil. Dread rumours of ghosts and ghouls, of meetings with earth-spirits, kept folk from straying into its shadowy depths. The sailors sat uneasily around a fire on the rim of the hollow. They would come no further and only fear of Gublak kept them from fleeing for their lives. Though the Urgils and the wolves had sidled closer in, the same sense of unease filled their hearts. But such a place suited the goblin well.

His consuming desire for the Star-Pearl led him to the blackest reaches of the hollow, where the dark had a deathliness of its own. His eyes burned green and in their light appeared many other pairs of pale eyes, hovering bodilessly in the murk.

Ulris gazed intently through half-lidded eyes as his master began to weave a spell. The sound of endless mournful sighings haunted his ears and a chill wind whirled about him. His fur prickled. He heard the faint cry of the goblin calling upon nameless dark powers. Then it seemed he dissolved into a ghastly green mist which ebbed into the earth. The wolf sat, mesmerized.

.   .   *   .   .

Peter stumbled through the thickening mist. He called to his companions but his voice sounded weak and muffled. He knew he must not panic and pinched himself hard. To run now would be disastrous. Slowly, he picked his way from tree to tree, clutching at the wet bark and trying to find safe places for his feet. The swampy ground smelt foul and he felt terribly heavy inside. This was a bad place to be.

He felt something move. Suddenly, a slimy tentacle whipped out of the swamp and snapped itself around his ankle. He fell with a loud splash. The mire began to heave and Peter cried out. He was being pulled towards a dark mound by some terrible unseen force. Vainly he thrashed around. A dank hole loomed ahead and with a rush of water and slime he was sent careering into its mouth.

He landed on his backside in a stinking pile of mud and leaves. With heart thumping fit to burst he staggered to his feet and looked around. Above his head hung hundreds of hairy roots. He could see no sign of the way by which he had entered. Ahead lay a tunnel lit by a faint grey phosphorescence. He thought he heard a noise, perhaps a cry, from somewhere along its length.

Very cautiously he crept forwards. Roots brushed at his face like giant living cobwebs. It was extremely cold and he shivered in his wet clothes.

Not far ahead the tunnel curved to the right. As Peter rounded the bend he received an awful shock. There, transfixed against the wall, hung Flip-flop, bound by dozens of roots which had wrapped themselves about his limbs. His eyes stared vacantly into space and Peter feared he must be dead. Vainly he tried to tear the roots away, but the more he pulled, with a horrid creaking sound, the tighter they gripped. He choked in despair and staggered blindly on.

Suddenly, the tunnel opened out into a cave and there to his horror he found his brother and sister and Princess Alena. They, like Flip-flop, did not move. But no tree roots held them. Instead, their bodies were fused to the grey rock and before his terrified gaze were slowly turning to stone. Already their legs and backs were cruelly transformed. His dear companions seemed destined to become nothing more than stone gargoyles staring helplessly from the harsh rock.

Peter's limbs grew leaden. He found he could no longer move his feet. Surely the same terrible fate awaited him. Then he heard a deep sinister voice.

'I am the Earth-Trog, devourer of the lost. You are mine for ever. None escape my grasp.'

Peter struggled with all his will. 'Well, you're not having me,' he cried defiantly.

The voice laughed, hollow and mocking. 'But I shall, for a bargain has been struck.'

'What bargain?'

'A certain goblin desires a certain jewel. For the price of your souls I have agreed to assist him. That is the bargain. Now that I have my spoil, he shall have his desire. You will become part of me. Resistance is useless.'

At that moment a green mist started to seep into the cavern. Peter stared aghast as it formed into a lurid emerald slime on the floor. Slowly it began to take on the familiar gruesome shape of Gublak. In wild panic Peter struggled and cried out.

Something in the back of his mind tried to speak through the terror, a clear, cool word, 'This will aid you should you need it.' He struggled to remember what it was but a sleepy cloud muffled his memory.

Then it came to him. His arms, though stiff, could still move. With a supreme effort of will he reached into his pocket and closed his fingers gratefully around the Ice Maiden's crystal. He struggled to draw it forth.

All the while the spirit of Gublak grew and grew before him until it assumed monstrous proportions. Peter was scared out of his wits. He managed to hold up the crystal but his heart quailed. To his dismay it began to melt between his fingers. The evil eyes of Gublak leered at his plight while the stone-cold grip of the Earth-Trog tightened about his limbs.

'No!' he gasped. 'Elmesh help me!'

The crystal was by now no more than the size of a pea and all hope seemed lost. Peter made one last desperate effort to conquer his fear. He thought of Oswain and the forest-folk. He remembered Aldred the stoat who had fearlessly come to their aid at the cost of his own life. A kind of shiver ran through his limbs. He set his jaw, and light began to shine from the crystal.

Slowly the stiffness eased from his limbs as his courage returned. He held the crystal high between thumb and forefinger. Its triumphant blaze filled the cave.

'Now we will see who is the stronger,' he cried. A mighty power filled his heart. He felt invincible as he approached the spectre of Gublak.

'Go, I command you in the name of Elmesh! You shall not have your desire. Begone now!'

The green image wavered and the face contorted in hatred, but with a hollow-sounding hiss it began to fade. Soon Peter stood alone. He smiled grimly.

'Earth-Trog, whatever you are, you cannot keep your bargain. You are denied your prey. Release these captives, lest I burn the very heart out of you.'

The Earth-Trog growled but did not obey.

The light from the crystal spattered red, and tongues of fire began to lick at the cavern walls. Hanging roots shrivelled and smouldered. The air grew hot. A loud roar echoed at last from the earth.

'Enough!'

Peter remained unrelenting. 'Set them free,' he commanded. 'I shall not cease until you obey.'

The Earth-Trog gave in. To Peter's relief he saw his companions come back to life. But he did not yet run to comfort them; his will was set upon holding the fearsome Earth-Trog in check.

'Release the rabbit,' he ordered.

Moments later Flip-flop came stumbling into the cave to join his dazed companions. They clearly had no idea of what was going on and seemed not to recognize Peter. He appeared to them as a knight in shining armour and bearing a blazing sword.

'Your power is matched, indeed mastered,' he declared. 'You will open a way to the earth above.'

'It shall be, for the moment, it shall be,' the voice rumbled.

There was a thunderous crash and one wall of the cavern split asunder revealing a slope which led to level grass and to a clear night sky.

'Follow me,' Peter ordered the others. Then, by the light of the crystal, he led them out to safety.

The earth shook and the rent closed. 'Vengeance!' was the last threatening word Peter heard from the Earth-Trog.

Through the trees and on to higher, drier ground he led his band until, at length, he called a halt. Only then did he return the crystal to his pocket, before sinking to the ground in an exhausted heap. The others came to themselves and recognized him.

'W. . .what happened?' asked Sarah. 'I feel as though I've just had a terrible dream. I fell down a hole and began to turn into stone. Then a shining knight came to rescue me. And . . . and here I am,' she ended lamely.

'I've had the same dream,' Princess Alena said quietly. 'Only I saw Gublak coming towards me to snatch the Star-Pearl. Then I, too, was rescued.' She felt anxiously for the jewel about her neck.

Andrew's experience was similar, while Flip-flop thought he had been buried alive and was turning into a carrot.

'What about you, Pete?' Andrew queried.

His brother gave a relieved laugh. 'Oh, something like yours, I suppose.' He was not sure whether to tell them everything or not. In fact, it seemed a bit of a dream to him now it was over.

'All I can say is, we've had a very close escape. You were not dreaming, any of you. We could easily have been killed in that swamp.' He gave Flip-flop a stern look. 'You know, you really are stupid not to have kept to the path. What would Oswain have said if you'd lost us all, eh? You're supposed to show us the way, not lead us into a mess.'

The rabbit looked suitably crestfallen. 'I'm sorry,'

he said. 'I suppose I didn't think about the dangers. I was more interested in finding those carrots.'

'Well, mind you don't make the same mistake again,' Princess Alena reprimanded him.

He nodded glumly. Somehow carrots didn't seem quite so important now.

'Can we get some sleep now?' Andrew pleaded. 'I feel as though I'm turning to stone.'

Peter glanced at him sharply. Andrew laughed, 'Oh, no, don't worry. Just tired, that's all!'

Everyone laughed and then they snuggled down together to snatch a few hours' sleep.

.   .   *   .   .

A tremor in the ground woke Andrew. He blinked and nudged the others. The sun was well up and the day looked promising.

'Wakey, wakey, everyone. Come on.'

'Oh, shush,' groaned Sarah. 'You're so noisy in the mornings, Andrew.'

'I know, but it's the only way to get you up,' he retorted.

The others stirred.

Their yawns and stretches were cut short by another tremor. Sarah looked anxiously at her elder brother.

'What do you think that is, Peter?'

'I'm not sure,' he replied slowly. 'But we made a new enemy under the ground yesterday, and he's not very happy with us. Come on, everyone. We need to be on our way—and fast!'

Chapter Sixteen

FLIGHT

All night long Ulris sat in that hideous hollow where the wraiths had their dwelling. Never once did he move but his bright yellow eyes were always alert, watching and waiting.

Dawn broke over the horizon and the blackness turned to cold, shadowy grey. There, motionless on the ground, lay the form of his master. The wolf arose and loped towards him. Gublak stirred as from a deep sleep.

Ulris gave him an enquiring look. 'Have you had good success, Eminence?' he asked.

'I have travelled the dark places of the earth and met with kindred spirits,' the goblin muttered. 'Dark and deliciously foul my paths have been—but no, I have not had success.' He spat the words angrily. 'So nearly in my grasp they were, again so close was my desire, but they possessed some fearful power which even I and the Earth-Trog together could not resist. I was forced into retreat.'

The wolf growled.

'But for those accursed children the Star-Pearl would be mine by now,' Gublak continued. 'If only that fool of a captain had not brought them to me. He must pay dearly for his folly!'

'Then the quest is lost?' the wolf asked. 'Shall we kill the captain now, before we return to the island, or after?'

'No,' screamed the goblin. 'Fool! We are not going back. I have not come this far to be thwarted at the last. We shall take up the chase. I must have that jewel. Do you not understand? I see nothing else in my dreams. I long for its power. What could I not do if I possessed it! And it is in the hands of a foolish girl who does not understand what she has. Pah!'

'But soon they will reach the Great Forest,' Ulris protested. 'You know what that means. We have no strength in that enchanted place.'

'Then we shall draw them out,' snarled Gublak. 'The captain and his crew shall be useful to that end. And when their blood is shed in battle it will be fitting reward for the trouble they have brought upon me.'

The wolf's eyes gleamed. 'Then we will take the girl?'

Gublak nodded. 'Together with our revenge upon those companions of hers. I shall see to it that their death is slow and painful.'

'I, too, shall avenge my dead,' growled Ulris. 'Yet what, Eminence, if the princess still refuses to willingly give you the Star-Pearl? You cannot take it by force.'

'Then she shall die,' said the goblin. His eyes blazed. 'If the Star-Pearl cannot be mine, then none shall have it. I have bargained with dark powers to possess it or destroy it. Whichever way, my reward will be great. Rouse them, Ulris. We march at once!'

.   .   *   .   .

Ominous rumblings from deep underground urged

133

the little band on. Even Flip-flop took the threat seriously. In fact, the only time he stopped was when he spotted some carrots growing by the roadside. Even earthquakes had to wait while he dealt with the serious business of breakfast!

'Something big is brewing up, I just feel it,' Peter puffed as they hastened up a lightly wooded hill.

'It's as though we've woken some sleeping underground giant,' said Sarah.

'You're not far wrong, I think,' he replied.

Andrew came trotting alongside. 'D'you think we're going to have an earthquake? You know, with the ground splitting open and swallowing us up, and all that? I keep getting ready to jump back. Or should I jump forwards?'

'Oh, be quiet, Andrew,' Peter said. 'This is no joke.' He turned round to where the princess was lagging behind. 'Come on, Alena. Get a move on, will you?'

'I'm doing the best I can,' she panted. 'And I'll thank you to treat a princess with more respect!'

'At least she's calling herself a princess again,' said Sarah. 'I hope it lasts.'

'Hm, she's still got to meet Oswain,' Peter replied. 'She doesn't seem very keen on the idea.'

'I'm not surprised,' Sarah retorted. 'She's expecting to be told off by her big brother. I don't like that either!'

The party reached the brow of the hill and before them stretched a vast sweeping valley. Rough grassland tumbled down in rolling slopes to the valley floor, where a sandy brown expanse took over. In the distance a silvery thread glinted in the sunshine.

'We've reached the waste plains,' Flip-flop explained. 'That's the River Wendle over there.'

'So that's the Great Forest beyond it?' Andrew pointed to the dark area which spread as far as the eye could see.

'That's correct,' Flip-flop acknowledged. 'We're nearly home.'

Just then the ground gave a sickening heave. A nearby tree toppled with a crash of branches and the skyline seemed to shake. The five companions clung to one another for support and waited fearfully until the tremor passed. Flip-flop clutched his stomach and wished he hadn't eaten so many carrots.

'It's getting worse,' said Peter. 'We must hurry. Come on, let's run down this bit.'

They dashed down the hillside into what they hoped was the safety of the valley. Flip-flop went onto all fours and fairly flew past everyone else. On and on they ran until the hill was far behind.

'Hang on. I've got a stitch,' Sarah gasped. 'Do you think it's safe to stop for a moment?'

'I don't think it's going to be safe until we get across the river,' said Peter. 'But all right.'

'I'm dying of thirst,' panted Princess Alena. 'Is there any water nearby?'

'As a matter of fact,' said Flip-flop with the air of one who knows, 'there's a stream just a bit further on.'

'Well, let's keep going until we reach it,' said Peter. 'We'll walk, okay?'

However, when they reached the spot where the stream should have been, to Flip-flop's consternation they found nothing but a dried up bed of stones.

'Odd,' he said. 'There's always water here. I wonder where it's gone?'

'Perhaps somebody's drunk it all,' suggested Andrew. 'Oh, well, we'll just have to go without, I suppose. At least the Wendle's got plenty of water in it—if we last out that long.'

The sun blazed hot and the air was sultry. It was

very quiet. Just occasionally faint rumblings could be heard in the distance. Nobody spoke much. It was enough just to keep going. And not a drop of water was to be found anywhere.

At length they reached the end of the grassland but unexpectedly found themselves at the edge of a sandy cliff which, through centuries of rain and frost, had been crumbling back to form the dun-coloured mud-flats which spread out below. Dirty streams, now dried up, had cut deep chasms across this barren landscape. It looked like something from another planet.

'Coo, talk about soil erosion,' said Andrew. 'This cliff must have been breaking down for years.'

'Can we get down it?' Princess Alena asked anxiously.

'Oh yes,' the rabbit replied. 'Get a bit dusty, that's all. Nothing to worry about.'

'What about the mud? Is it soft or what?' Peter queried.

'Not at this time of year. It's fairly dry and you can walk on it,' Flip-flop reassured him.

'You'd better be right this time,' Peter warned.

The party began a cautious descent down the shallowest bit they could find. It was very slippery with nothing to grab on to. By the time they had slithered down to the bottom everyone was covered in brown dust.

Much to their relief, Flip-flop was right about the mud. It was quite firm, though squelchy in places, and although they had to jump the cracks they made good progress.

'Next stop the river,' said Peter cheerfully. He was beginning to feel relieved. 'I think we're out of trouble now.'

But he spoke too soon. Minutes later, a fearsome

roar from behind made everyone spin round. The cliff down which they had so recently come seemed to explode before their eyes. They watched awe-struck as a vast surge of black mire erupted from its length and poured towards them like a huge tidal wave.

'It's the Earth-Trog's revenge,' cried Peter. 'We'll be swamped alive. Run for it. Run for your lives!'

Nobody needed a second bidding. They fled for the safety of the river, urged on by the crashing roar of the flood which bore down upon them.

Suddenly, Andrew, who was in front, came teeter-ing to a halt.

'There's the river,' he shouted. 'But we've got to get down this. Look!'

He stood on the brink of another small cliff. It would only take five minutes to descend it. But they didn't have five minutes.

'We'll never do it,' Sarah screamed as she and the others joined him.

They looked back in panic at the relentless black wave which was pouring across the mud-flats to-wards them. There was nothing they could do to avoid its path.

All seemed lost. Then, suddenly the air was rent by a shrill screech. Everyone looked up. It was Sarah who first recognized the magnificent white eagle winging towards them at an incredible speed.

'It's Arca!' she cried. 'Look! He's come to rescue us!'

Moments later the great bird streaked in to land. He wasted not a moment.

'On my back,' he cawed. 'One at a time. Hasten now.'

'You first, Alena,' Peter ordered. She protested that it should be Sarah but Peter was firm. 'Look, don't argue. You're the one we're supposed to be rescuing. Now get on.'

He gave her an unceremonious shove and she clutched desperately at the eagle's neck as he immediately took to the air. The others watched as the bird swooped low across the river and deposited the princess safely on the other side.

'Thank goodness for that,' sighed Peter. 'You next Sarah. And don't you argue either.'

Sarah leapt astride the eagle and rubbed his head affectionately. 'Just like old times,' she laughed as they took off.

He took Andrew and Flip-flop together on the next trip, holding the petrified rabbit in his beak. Peter anxiously hopped from one foot to the other. The surging swamp, over twice his height, was scarcely twenty metres away as Arca set out towards him.

It was surely too late. As the wave reached him it reared up and Peter saw it take on the vile form of some primeval swamp monster. Baleful eyes glared hatred and death as the Earth-Trog prepared to crush him. Its great shadow blotted out the sky.

But Arca sped under the towering wave as it crashed down. Summoning all his strength and speed, the mighty bird seized Peter in his powerful talons and whisked him away to safety in the nick of time. The black mass spent its force and poured harmlessly over the cliff.

'Phew, that was close,' Peter gasped. 'Thanks, Arca. You were just in time.'

'I was in Elmesh's time. That is always sufficient,' the eagle replied.

Peter was reunited with his companions to great whoops of joy. He marvelled how Arca had not hurt him when those fearsome talons had gripped him.

'Fantastic!' cried Andrew. 'What a rescue.' He danced a jig and made faces at the dark mud across the river.

The others crowded around Arca, chattering nineteen to the dozen. Except for Flip-flop, that is, who didn't trust eagles and kept his distance. Arca might just be a bit peckish!

Just then a tall, lean figure stepped unnoticed from behind a tree. He stood watching the merriment with a smile on his rugged face.

'Hail, friends,' he called.

The babble ceased at the sound of his voice and all turned to see who spoke.

'Why, it's Oswain!' cried Sarah with delight. She raced across and threw her arms around him. 'It's so wonderful to see you again,' she whispered.

'You too, Sarah,' he replied. 'I've waited many days for this moment. Greetings, Peter. And you, Andrew. Flip-flop, I'll see you later!'

The boys shook hands warmly with their old friend. Then he looked at the princess. She shambled awkwardly towards him, with her eyes lowered.

'So, you are my sister, Alena,' he breathed. 'After all these years. Come, do not be afraid. I will not bite you! This is a day for great rejoicing. It is not every day my sister pays me a visit.'

He held out his hand to her as she approached. The others watched with bated breath to see how she would respond. She reached him and clasped his hand tight, then looked up earnestly into his face.

'I'm sorry,' she said.

Chapter Seventeen

OLD FRIENDS

Peter, Sarah and Andrew walked well ahead of Oswain and Princess Alena as they entered the beautiful paths of the Great Forest. Flip-flop led the way.

Everywhere flowers burst from the banks in dazzling displays of colour. Carpets of blue, red and yellow ran riot among the trees. Heady scents wafted in the light breeze and overhead dappled sunlight fell through a canopy of fresh greenery. Stolid oaks and stately elms, ladylike birches and sweeping willows graced their path. Countless birds sang their welcoming praises in the warm summer air.

'Oh, this is so gorgeous,' exclaimed Sarah. 'Far better even than when we were last here.'

'Well, everything has had time to grow, hasn't it?' said Peter. 'Quite a bit different from when we first arrived. D'you remember how dead it all was?'

'Yes, and then we got caught and thought the animals were the enemy,' Andrew reminded them. 'We couldn't have been more wrong if we'd tried,' he laughed.

'Still, all that's changed for ever,' said Peter. 'Oswain's seen to that.'

Andrew wanted to know what the others thought

would happen now they had reached the Great Forest.

'Oh, I expect Oswain will take Alena back home and we'll go back to ours,' Peter answered.

'What about Gublak? D'you think he's dead?'

'Maybe,' Peter replied somewhat vaguely. He was not quite sure what had happened in the Earth-Trog's lair.

'I don't know,' said Sarah. 'I've got this funny feeling that it's not all over yet.'

'It's certainly not all over for me,' Flip-flop declared. 'I still have to answer to Oswain, don't forget.' He looked glum.

'Oh, don't worry,' said Andrew. 'I expect we'll put a good word in for you—even though you were a bit of a twit! After all, you did get us here in the end.'

So their carefree chatter continued as they wended their way through the forest. Soon they drew near the dwellings of the forest-folk. To the children's delight everybody came out to meet them and before long they were surrounded by a hustling, chattering crowd of foxes, stoats, weasels, rabbits, badgers, squirrels, hedgehogs and just about every other woodland creature imaginable. By the time they reached the centre of the village it was almost impossible to move for the crush.

Many of the older animals remembered Peter, Sarah and Andrew and shouted their greetings. Most of the younger ones were simply curious to see these strange creatures of whom their stories spoke and nagged the grown-ups to tell the old tales again.

'This is just amazing,' Peter laughed. 'What a sight!'

Suddenly, the hubbub dropped and, with much 'shushing', the crowd drew back respectfully so that a way opened before the children. Everyone watched as an elderly badger, leaning on a walking stick, shuffled towards them, assisted by two young attendants.

'Trotter!' cried Peter. He ran to him and hugged him affectionately. Sarah and Andrew beamed all over their faces and greeted their old friend warmly.

'My, oh, my,' he quavered. 'I never did expect to meet you again, my dear friends. What a delightful surprise it was when I heard you were in our realm once more. Elmesh be praised that I have lived to see it.'

'It's absolutely wonderful to see you again, Trotter,' Sarah enthused.

'Well, my dears,' the badger went on. 'You find me not so young as I used to be. Or Mrs Trotter for that matter. Oh, yes, she is still alive and well,' he re-assured them as he saw worried looks cross their faces. 'But age takes its toll, you know. She is resting at home.'

Peter was a bit puzzled. 'But how long is it since we were last here?' he asked. 'It wasn't that long ago for us.'

'Oh dear, yes, I forget that strange things happen when you pass the barrier between one realm and another.' He chuckled to himself and wheezed a little. 'Why, Peter, I have seen sixteen summers since last you came.'

'Sixteen years! So that's why we never heard about Alena before,' said Andrew. 'She wasn't even born. I've been wondering about that ever since we found out who she was.'

'But Oswain doesn't look any older,' said Sarah.

'Oswain never appears to age,' said the badger with a twinkle in his eye. 'No, he just seems to grow wiser as the summers pass. But now, all this excitement is enough for me. You must come and meet the wife.'

He motioned the crowd to be about their business. 'Take my arm would you, Peter? Not too hasty, though.'

'What about Oswain and Alena?' Peter asked.

'They will join us soon, I expect. I imagine they wish to be alone for the moment.'

The party wound slowly to Trotter's delightful old cottage. Nothing seemed to have changed much, except that the grounds were well-tended nowadays.

'This place is so full of memories,' Sarah sighed as they crossed the oak-beamed porch.

'Come on now, in here,' said the badger. He led them into the front room.

'Why, m'dears, how lovely to see you again,' cried Mrs Trotter. She sat in an old sofa with her feet up and a blanket wrapped round her legs. 'I've had the kettle on ever since I knew you were coming. Sit yourselves down and make yourselves comfy. We've so much to talk about.'

The children greeted her warmly and soon they were busily chatting together about old times. They became so engrossed in conversation that they didn't even hear Oswain and Princess Alena come in.

'I see you have renewed your acquaintance,' he laughed. 'A good day, eh, Trotter?'

The old badger nodded and mumbled something appropriate through a mouthful of biscuit.

Oswain and the princess sat down. Sarah was glad to see she was smiling.

'Now,' said the ruler of the forest. 'You must tell us all that has befallen you. Some matters I have seen from afar and some I have gleaned from Alena during our walk. But I would hear your tale from the beginning.'

Peter began and, with the help of Sarah and Andrew, told of their entry into the kingdom and

143

their capture by the pirates and Gublak. Oswain smiled when they told him of the old shepherd.

'That was strange,' Sarah pondered. 'I sensed he was friendly somehow and I almost thought I knew him. But it's still a mystery who he is.'

'Do you not know?' Trotter chuckled. 'Why, it was Oswain himself.'

'What?' said the three in unison.

'But how?' asked Peter.

'It was a vision you saw,' Oswain explained.

'But why were you not as yourself . . . I mean . . . as we would recognize you?' Peter wanted to know.

'Sarah very nearly did,' Oswain replied. 'The reason is not hard to understand. In the enchanted glade we learned from Elmesh of your plight but, much as we would have wished, we were not permitted to come to your aid. Yet I was allowed to give you a little guidance at times.'

'I still don't get why you appeared in disguise,' said Andrew.

'Let me ask you a question. What have you most needed on your journey?' Oswain asked.

'Hope and courage,' Peter said promptly, recalling the Ice Maiden's words.

Oswain nodded. 'If you had recognized who I was, you would have expected far more of me than I was permitted to give. And in your disappointment, your hearts would have failed you. What then would have become of hope?'

'I see,' said Peter, but he was not altogether sure that he did.

Andrew changed the subject. 'Anyway, thanks for helping us 'cos we really needed it at the time.' He recounted how they had escaped and told of their meeting with the treacherous Dringol.

Sarah noticed Oswain's interest quicken when they

spoke of the Ice Maiden. 'Hey, Peter, have you still got that crystal?' she queried.

He dug into his pocket. 'Yes, here it is.'

'Well, I think Oswain should have it,' she said firmly.

Peter had no objections and handed it over. Oswain gazed in wonder at the jewel.

'This is a stone of destiny,' he murmured. 'I must surely seek out this Ice Maiden of whom you tell.'

'Why don't you have the stone set in a ring?' Sarah suggested.

He looked directly at her with a questioning gaze but her face was a picture of smiling innocence.

'Maybe I shall,' he said thoughtfully.

Their tale continued and the shadows began to lengthen in the golden glow of sunset. Peter looked out of the leaded window.

'Can we visit Aldred's memorial?' he asked.

'By all means,' Oswain smiled. 'And then, on to the enchanted glade, eh?'

'Oh, yes please,' they chorused.

'I will stay here if you don't mind,' said Trotter. 'But do return to us and stay the night, won't you? Beds have been prepared for everyone.'

They thanked Mr and Mrs Trotter for their hospitality and then made their way to Aldred's memorial. There, before the statue of the heroic stoat, they stood in solemn silence.

Oswain ushered the children away and led them in the direction of the enchanted glade. A tingling sense of expectancy filled them as they approached the sentinel stones which marked the entrance to the glade. The air buzzed with life and when they passed the stones a golden glory momentarily blinded their eyes as the last rays of the setting sun blazed their trail across the glen.

The first stars of evening came peeking out from the blue canopy above as the five approached Elmere, the Star-Pool, alongside which rested the famed Merestone. Each one felt the awesome power of the place and their voices were hushed.

'This is where I learned your plight and sought to bend my will to your aid,' Oswain whispered.

'It's so special,' Sarah said. 'There's nowhere else like it in all the world.' She wanted to say more, but there were no words to express all that was in her heart.

'Often I come here to learn the ways of Elmesh,' said Oswain. 'You speak truly, Sarah. It is a place of wonder.'

Each of the three children took their turn to look into the enchanted pool but, slightly to their disappointment, they saw only their own faces.

'It is not for you to see visions this night,' Oswain said. 'But, Alena, you may see many things by El-la's light.'

The princess did not reply. She was overwhelmed by the enchantment of the place and gazed in wonder at the pearl-like drops of water which fell into the glowing pool.

'I wish we could stay the night here,' said Sarah wistfully. 'I could live for ever in this place.'

Oswain smiled. 'I am sure you could, Sarah, but you must not neglect the hospitality of Mr and Mrs Trotter.' He glanced at the evening sky. 'Soon it will be dark and El-la will have risen. You must return to their cottage.'

'Aren't you coming with us?' Andrew asked.

Oswain shook his head. 'Not as yet. Nor Alena. For we must speak alone of many things and see what we shall see in this place. Mind your steps now, but you shall find the way with ease.'

The three children reluctantly did as they were bidden and departed from the enchanted glade.

'D'you think Oswain's going to tell Alena off?' asked Andrew.

'No, I doubt it somehow,' his brother replied. 'I expect he'll make her completely well and sort everything out. That's why she was meant to come here, I reckon.'

'Oh well, that's about it for us, I suppose,' Sarah sighed. 'We've done what we were sent for. But I can't help feeling that there's . . .'

She never finished her sentence. A rough hand clamped over her mouth and she was pulled to the ground by two dark figures.

Before Peter and Andrew could do anything to help other shadowy shapes darted from the undergrowth and leapt upon them. They scuffled and struggled with all their might. Andrew was no match for his assailants and was soon held captive. Peter put up a good fight but a blow on the back of his head sent him reeling into unconsciousness.

'Well done, me hearties,' hissed a voice. 'Tie 'em up and let's be out of here. Reckon Cap'n Gaspar and 'is Eminence'll be 'ighly pleased with tonight's catch.'

Chapter Eighteen

THE PAST REVEALED

'See, El-la has risen,' said Oswain. He directed Princess Alena's attention to the bright star which hung low in the sky yet greatly outshone its companions. The enchanted glade seemed to become even more alive beneath its brilliance, and the pearl-like drops of water which fed the Star-Pool from the rock above gleamed in response.

Oswain spoke solemnly to his adopted sister. 'The time has come for you to know the truth about yourself, Alena. You are a child of destiny, as I am myself. Long years ago I gazed into this same pool and discovered my fate. It was not easy.'

The princess returned his look. 'I don't think I am afraid,' she said. 'But would you hold my hand, please?'

He smiled and took it in his own. Together they approached the enchanted pool. Princess Alena felt a mixture of curiosity and awe as she leaned over the water and looked in.

At first she saw only her own reflection. Then the waters swirled and pictures began to form. A landscape unfolded before her and she heard a rushing noise as her eye raced over fields and rivers, across plains and mountains, until it came to rest on a stern northern land of craggy peaks and broad lakes. Imposing castles, mighty fortresses and vast cities were arrayed before her. This was a rich and proud kingdom.

In a moment, the vision changed and she saw a strong, tall man clothed in diamond-studded black leather and seated upon a magnificent throne. His features were as proud and stern as the land over which he ruled. The princess could feel the power of his personality reach right into her. Something stirred in her heart and she wondered at the greatness of this man to whom surely mighty empires bowed down.

A fair young woman, great with child, stood beside him. She was soon to give birth.

'It is Surin of Traun,' whispered Oswain. 'The most powerful dark lord of the Northern realms.'

The scene changed and they saw that a girl child had been born. Now the mighty ruler stood in a dimly-lit room, holding the baby before his gods. A black crow was perched upon his shoulder. Princess Alena heard the words within her mind.

'To the dark powers of Kraan I dedicate this child and call her Astar. By my oath, a mighty queen shall she be, invincible as I. The lands of the West shall be her domain. They will serve your power and bow before my rule.'

The princess looked in wonder. She caught a glimpse of the child's mother peering around the door with anguish written on her face.

The waters swirled once more and she could see the fair mother fleeing for her life with her baby clutched tightly to her. Fear and dread filled her face. The journey seemed unending until at last it brought her to a city which Princess Alena recognized as Elmar. Still the woman fled, twisting and turning among the narrow streets and always glancing behind her, until she came within sight of the palace gates.

Yet, even as she made to enter, two strangely-robed figures emerged from the shadows, one tall and lean, the other short and round.

A knife flashed from the hand of the taller one and Princess Alena gasped as she watched it plunge between the shoulder blades of the fugitive woman. She cried out and fell dead. One of the assailants rushed to seize the child but before he could do so, the palace guards came running and the two figures withdrew again into the shadows.

The baby girl was still alive and Princess Alena stared transfixed as she saw her borne into the palace.

In a final vision, the King and Queen of Elmar stood before the Lord Chancellor. The baby was in the Queen's arms. The princess heard the adoption order read and saw the Star-Pearl placed about the child's neck. A crow perched nearby. There could be no doubt that the child born to Surin was none other than Princess Alena herself.

The scene faded until she could see only her own face in the water. Strange emotions filled her heart. At last she knew who she was. Her name was Astar. She thought of the proud warrior king in all his splendour—her father—the man Oswain called Surin. She felt the awesome power of his oath to the dark gods.

Then the treachery of her mother's death angered her. Yet why had she fled to the Western capital in the first place? Perhaps the gods had dictated her steps. Would they have their way no matter what? Was the princess *meant* to serve their ends? Then what of the Star-Pearl? Was it to help her or was it a barrier to her true destiny?

Oswain released her hand and drew back. His face was grim.

'Then you are Astar, the offspring of Surin,' he said gravely. 'He is the sworn enemy of my family and of our kingdoms. By rights I should have you slain, yet here you stand as my sister. What strange fortune this is.'

The princess was trembling. 'I don't understand all this,' she said. 'If only I had not looked into the pool!'

'The revelations of the Star-Pool are not always a comfort, but nonetheless they serve great purposes,' Oswain answered. 'I pity you, Princess, for the choice which lies before you.'

She looked perplexed, so he explained, 'For many long years the house of Surin of Traun has plagued the Wester Lands. The king, your real father, is a great man; he is ambitious and ruthless. His empire is mighty, but he is not satisfied. Nor are the gods of Kraan whom he serves. Their baleful influence reached through him into my own country years ago and corrupted even the one I loved. I am no friend of Surin!'

Princess Alena had grown pale.

'Since then,' he continued, 'our strength has increased and we dwell secure. Surin cannot break the power of Elmesh which guards our borders. Yet times may change. The rule of my father has been long and wise, but, alas, he ages and must go the way of all mortal creatures.'

'And Surin, my real father, knows this?' Princess Alena asked.

'Indeed,' replied Oswain.

'Then won't you reign in his place, since you are the eldest?'

'My family has chosen to reign only in accord with

Elmesh's will. Thus, I was destined to rule the vast Eastern lands of the Great Forest. Yet who will fill the throne of Elmar when my father passes?' He gave the princess a penetrating look. 'It was to be you, Alena. Indeed, I see now that it shall be you. But as friend or foe? That is the question.'

Princess Alena looked aghast at her brother. The truth had dawned. She was indeed a daughter of destiny. Even now the conflict arose in her heart. Should she serve her father, Surin, in accordance with his oath? Or should she choose the way of her adoptive parents and reign in alliance with Oswain? Whatever her choice, one or other of them would become her mortal enemy.

'I don't know how to answer that question,' she sighed. 'What will become of me? And where does Gublak fit into all this?'

Oswain looked sadly upon the girl. 'I believe I can now answer your last question. As I gazed into the Star-Pool, seeking to bring you aid from afar, I learned that someone had plied Gublak with many favours and at last bewitched him so that he would covet the Star-Pearl more than anything else in the world.

'I did not know then who it was, but I know now that it is Surin, your father, who is behind all this. He has waited all these years until you should come of age. Now he seeks to make his move. Crow was his avenue to you and it was he who planted the seeds of rebellion which made you run away from home. Gublak did the rest.'

'But why does everyone want to get the Star-Pearl off me?' Princess Alena wailed. 'I don't even know why I have it. Gublak said it was worthless to me and . . .'

'He was lying,' Oswain interrupted. 'Greed always

leads to deceit, and he tried to fool you into thinking the jewel was unimportant.'

'But he wanted to use it himself,' said the princess. 'Would it have worked?'

Oswain shook his head. 'No, the Star-Pearl will serve only the will of Elmesh. It would be useless to Gublak. But the bewitchment does not let him know that. So he desires it still. Your father wanted him to take it from you because then you would no longer be protected from him and the powers he serves.'

Princess Alena was silent. She thought again of her real father. He was a magnificent warrior king and she knew his blood ran in her veins. Visions of grandeur passed before her. She saw herself standing with him and imagined his pride in her, Queen Astar, ruler of the West. Gublak had lied; she was of royal blood anyway. Only the Star-Pearl kept her from living as the daughter of Surin.

Then she thought of her adoptive parents. Deep down she loved them and she could see how they had pitied her and shown great kindness. She looked upon the strong face of Oswain and felt the wealth of goodness which flowed from him and all his domain. She could see now that it was her father's blood which had made her wary of him.

Oswain spoke again. 'My parents gave you the Star-Pearl not just to protect you from danger,' he said. 'They did not even know who your parents were. They bestowed it upon you to make you truly one of the royal family, Alena. They had no other children besides me so they looked upon you as a gift from Elmesh and chose you as heir to the throne. The jewel gives you the right and power to reign with Elmesh's blessing. Do you see its importance? It is the very key to the throne.'

She nodded but said nothing.

'You are now fifteen years of age,' Oswain continued. 'For you, it is the age of decision. You must choose freely whether to accept the Star-Pearl and serve Elmesh or to relinquish it and serve your father, Surin. It will be no easy decision, for many destinies turn upon it and much conflict will follow.'

'I must think,' the princess replied. 'But not in this place. For here I could easily choose to serve Elmesh but I cannot say it would be so when I left.'

Oswain nodded. 'Then let us depart and return to Mr and Mrs Trotter's house. There you may consider your decision in private.'

.　　.　　*　　.　　.

It didn't take them long to reach the badger's cottage and they were silent all the way.

Upon their arrival they were surprised to see lights in the window.

'Thank Elmesh you have returned,' exclaimed Trotter as they entered. 'I could not sleep and I feared some misadventure had befallen you.'

'No, we are quite safe,' Oswain smiled. 'But thank you for your concern, my friend. Are the children safely tucked up?'

'Are they not with you?' gasped the badger.

Oswain shook his head. Trotter staggered to an armchair. He sat down weakly.

'Oh dear,' he wheezed. 'Then something has gone terribly amiss. I knew it. We haven't seen them since they left with you.'

Oswain looked grim. He glanced sharply at Princess Alena. 'I suspect the work of Gublak. It seems his evil has penetrated even the sacred reaches of the Great Forest.'

He turned to the badger. 'Trotter, rest here, old friend, and do not trouble yourself. I must rouse the forest-folk. You come with me too, Alena. I do not want you out of my sight!'

They rushed from the cottage and hastened to the village dwellings. It didn't take long to gather a large crowd of animals in the centre, although there was much yawning and murmuring. Oswain swiftly explained what had happened and the muttering ceased.

'Find out what you can and return here,' he urged, 'and quickly. We have little time to lose.'

At once the loyal animals sped in all directions to search for tracks.

It didn't prove difficult to find where the scuffle had occurred, and the information was swiftly relayed to Oswain by a hare named Fleetfoot.

'Call my guard,' Oswain commanded.

Minutes later he was joined by a senior weasel called Stiggle and three illustrious mice named Fumble, Mumble and Grumble. Not that the mice lived up to their names any more. Years of patient training had turned them into quite a respectable guard of honour, with just occasional lapses, which amused the younger animals.

Oswain filled them in on the night's events. 'Stiggle, you and I will go with Fleetfoot to see what has been found. Fumble, Mumble and Grumble, you are to stay here with the princess. Do not let her out of your sight and especially do not let her remove the jewel she wears about her neck. Is that understood?'

'The matter is perfectly clear, sir,' answered Mumble.

'It will be our delight,' smiled Grumble, while Fumble saluted smartly.

A cluster of animals met Oswain and Stiggle when

they arrived at the scene with Fleetfoot. He pointed a way through the damaged undergrowth.

'That's where they've dragged them,' said Stiggle. 'We must follow their trail. But keep your eyes open, everyone. The enemy may still be about.'

Very stealthily the animals followed the scent. The excitement of the chase soon caught some of the younger ones and they hared ahead, but they were brought to an abrupt halt at a ford in the river and had to wait for the others. A lot of muddy footprints showed that this was where the brigands had crossed.

'Do we carry on, sir?' puffed Stiggle as he and Oswain reached the ford.

'Yes, but with greater care,' Oswain replied. He glanced at the sky. 'It is not long till dawn and there is little cover over the river. Tell some of the animals to return and fetch weapons. I have a feeling we shall need them before the day is very old.'

Half the group did this while the rest accompanied Oswain. They were soon within range of the enemy camp. The glow of a fire gave it away. Oswain motioned everyone to stop.

'We must wait for weapons,' he whispered to Stiggle. 'The goblin will have wolves prowling the camp. It's no use attacking like this. Let's just hope the children are still all right.'

The weasel agreed. 'Then let's leave the trail and make our way around to the higher ground on the right. That'll give us a little bit of surprise. Our folk will find us easily enough when they return with the arms.

.   .   *   .   .

Back in the village the three mice sat on the ground

with the princess. She looked glum. Fumble, Mumble and Grumble exchanged glances.

'Perhaps you should tell her a joke, Grumble,' suggested Fumble.

'Well, you might as well do cartwheels then,' he replied.

'Personally I would rather be asleep,' interjected Mumble. He addressed the princess. 'Er, um, what is your name, may I ask?'

'It is Alena,' she answered shortly. 'But you should call me, "Your Royal Highness".'

'Oh, um, yes, yerolines,' he mumbled, a bit put off.

That put paid to conversation for a good long while until, all of a sudden, the princess leapt to her feet. The mice jerked in surprise and Fumble fell over as he tried to rise too quickly.

'I don't feel I like the idea of being kept a prisoner, particularly by mice,' she declared haughtily. 'I shall take a walk.'

'I'm sorry, er, your royal highness,' said Grumble, 'but we've got our orders and we're to stay here with you.'

'I should look over there first, if I were you,' said the princess and she pointed with her finger behind them. The three mice turned and fell for the oldest trick in the book. In a flash the princess was off.

'Quick, she's making a bolt for it,' cried Grumble. 'After her!'

But whether it was Fumble's fault or not, the three of them collided and fell into a complaining heap on the ground. By the time they had untangled themselves, the princess had got clean away.

Chapter Nineteen

ALENA CHOOSES

Black-cloaked night was changing to grey-mantled dawn as Oswain surveyed the scene from the low, bushy hill where he and his party crouched on the north side of Gublak's camp. They were nearer than he had first imagined and he could plainly make out the prowling wolves, as well as pirates and Urgils. But what immediately caught his attention were three stakes to which were tied three figures. He guessed at once they were Peter, Sarah and Andrew. Stiggle moved up alongside him to take a look.

Before the weasel could comment they heard a disturbance behind them. Fearing the worst, they retreated hastily to their companions, only to be greeted by the sight of two distressed mice, desperately trying to catch their breath.

'What is it?' Oswain demanded. 'What has happened?'

'Isprinceslenashescaped,' gasped Mumble.

Grumble tutted impatiently. 'The princess, sir. She's run off, I'm sorry, sir.'

Oswain groaned.

'Where's Fumble?' Stiggle demanded. 'I suppose he's fallen over his tail somewhere!'

'No, he hasn't,' Grumble replied in defence of his

friend. 'He's gone after the princess. We've run straight here.'

Between them they quickly explained what had happened.

'We left Fumble to follow her trail after we crossed the ford,' said Mumble who had now regained control of his tongue.

'Then she's making for the enemy camp, I reckon,' Stiggle said.

Oswain agreed and dashed back through the bushes to his vantage point. And from there he could make out the slim figure of Princess Alena running straight towards Gublak's camp.

'We've got to stop her somehow,' hissed Stiggle who had just rejoined him.

'Yes,' said Oswain and made to rise. But something seemed to check him. He spoke grimly and Stiggle wondered at the seriousness of his tone. 'No, she must choose for herself. I must not force her. Let the princess face the goblin alone and decide her fate!'

.　　.　　*　　.　　.

Peter, Sarah and Andrew had fared badly since their capture by the pirates. They had been bound and gagged, then humped roughly through the forest, across the ford and on into Gublak's presence.

The goblin was delighted with the catch and immediately ordered the children to be tied to the stakes.

His green eyes flashed in the firelight as he addressed them. He spoke smoothly. 'I would have preferred the princess herself. But no matter. You will be useful in the bargaining. The Star-Pearl in exchange for your lives, eh? I do not think there will be much resistance.'

The children were quite helpless and entirely at the mercy of the goblin. Despair engulfed them as he left them for his tent. A prowling wolf brushed against Sarah's leg and she gave a muffled scream from behind her gag. Andrew stared blankly at the pirates and the Urgils gathered around the fire. It would be a long night.

For Peter especially the hours dragged by with agonizing slowness. From the moment he regained consciousness his head had not ceased to throb. He would have done anything just to have been able to rub the bruise. All night long he battled with the sickening pain and a despondency which almost overwhelmed him. He dare not lose heart. Help must come from somewhere.

Dawn brought little relief from the discomfort but it made him feel a little better. Oswain would find a way to rescue them, he felt sure. After all, this was not the first time they had been in a tight spot.

He was just regaining confidence when, to his dismay, he saw Princess Alena running alone towards the camp. She could not know she was heading for trouble, he thought. He tried to warn her, but the gag stopped him producing anything more than a muffled grunt.

The princess slowed to a walk, then to his amazement, strode boldly right into the centre of the encampment. Her arrival caused quite a commotion and the goblin himself emerged from his tent to see what all the fuss was about. An oily smile lit up his fat face when he saw who it was.

'Ah, Princess, so you have come to me at last. You will see that your friends have already joined us.' He glanced towards the children. 'It has been a long time since we last spoke and I have eagerly awaited this moment.' His voice took on a steely edge. 'I need hardly tell an intelligent girl such as yourself what my terms are.'

Peter stared wide-eyed at the princess. He willed her to flee even though it didn't look as if she had a chance. If only he could do something. She glanced coldly in the direction of the bound children, then back to Gublak.

Only then did it dawn on Peter that Princess Alena may have chosen, after all, to flee the forest and join forces with Gublak. Oswain would never have sent her unprotected like this. In fact, he was nowhere to be seen. Peter groaned within himself.

Just then, he felt an odd movement behind him. Someone was tugging at his bonds. Peter jumped with surprise and tried to twist his head to see who it was.

'Keep still,' hissed a voice. 'It's me, Fumble. Pretend nothing's happening and look straight ahead.'

Peter could have shouted for joy and really had to fight hard not to give the game away. Fumble seemed to take ages gnawing at the knots, but actually it was only a matter of moments before the intrepid mouse succeeded. To Peter's intense relief, his bonds fell away.

.   .   *   .   .

Princess Alena's mind had been in a whirl since she had looked into the Star-Pool. The knowledge of who she really was and the awful choice which lay before her had left her completely dazed; a thousand conflicting thoughts had battled away in her head, and she really did not know what to do next.

It was the discovery of the children's capture which

had helped her make up her mind. It meant Gublak was nearby, presumably just across the river. She had determined then to escape and get to him. For Princess Alena knew with terrible certainty that the only way she could make her decision was to come face to face with the goblin.

Evading the three mice had proved all too easy. She fled in the general direction of the river, prepared to swim across if necessary. But she found the ford and was soon on the other bank. From the footprints and broken twigs lying around, it had not been difficult for her to find the way from there on.

The sun was just beginning to light the sky behind her as she entered Gublak's camp.

'Give me the Star-Pearl,' the goblin now demanded. 'Let me have it and your friends go free. You may join me or go your way, as you wish. But the Star-Pearl must be mine.'

His eyes glittered greedily and he watched as she slowly drew forth the jewel from her bosom so that it hung in view about her neck on its silver chain.

'Ah, how beautiful it is,' he sighed. 'No use to you, of course. But beautiful to me. Any reward you ask shall be yours, Princess. Only let me possess it.'

At this point Princess Alena felt nothing but loathing for the goblin's greed and was about to refuse him, when a very strange thing began to happen.

As she beheld the revolting creature, his whole appearance started to change and in place of his fat green figure, she saw the tall, stern form of Surin. She gasped with shock. Her head reeled. Gublak was not Surin—was he? Surely not!

Yet it was without doubt Surin's steely eyes which seemed to bore right through her. She tried to move, but her legs would not obey. She was spellbound.

'Take off the Star-Pearl,' the voice ordered. 'Give it

to the goblin. You are my child. Astar is your name, and as the daughter of Surin shall you be known.' The figure's lips curled into a smile. 'The gods of Kraan have directed your destiny well. Now the time has come for you to rule, my child. Long enough have you been slave to the contemptible ways of the Wester kingdom. Remove this chain, cast off this trash, and all will bow to serve your will.'

'Yes, father,' the princess answered meekly. 'I will do as you say.'

All eyes were upon her as she reached behind her neck for the clasp.

None who viewed the transformation or who heard the strange voice from Gublak's lips understood what it all meant, least of all the three children. But Peter realized that some sort of enchantment had taken place. He also knew that there was only one chance left. Without any further thought, he took it, and hurled himself at the figure.

His arms wrapped around the legs and he brought Gublak (for it was, of course, Gublak after all) crashing to the ground with a rugby tackle worthy of the first team. So unexpected was his action that it was done before anyone could stop him. The goblin howled with rage.

In an instant, Peter was surrounded. Ulris stood panting over him, his breath foul and his jaws slavering. The wolf glanced at his master who was struggling to his feet. He awaited the order to tear Peter's throat out. Gublak was breathing heavily as he rose. His eyes were hard but he held out a restraining hand in the wolf's direction. The bewitched goblin was quite unaware that Surin had spoken through him. He assumed Princess Alena was simply giving in to his demands.

'One moment, Ulris,' he grated. 'Your foolish

friend tries my patience, Princess. He thinks to prevent what must be. But he has failed. Now, the Star-Pearl, if you please.'

Princess Alena was as amazed as anyone at Peter's sudden attack. On the surface it seemed such a hopeless gesture. Yet it had not been in vain. The vision of Surin was gone and the spell broken. Something stirred powerful within her at that moment. She faced Gublak squarely.

'No! The jewel shall not be yours.' Her voice rang out across the dell and her eyes shone with a new light. 'Hear this, all you powers,' she proclaimed. 'Astar I shall never be. Surin I renounce. I, Alena, accept the Star-Pearl. I shall serve Elmesh!'

An angry rumble of thunder sounded far away in the north, though only the keenest ears heard it.

At once, an amazing transformation took place before everyone's astonished gaze. The princess seemed to be lost in an envelope of bright blue light and the air filled with a strange music. As the light slowly faded, gone were her tattered travelling clothes and she was clad in shimmering silver-blue and a tiara adorned her golden hair.

Gublak and his evil band looked on in horror. Peter had tears in his eyes as he gazed from where he lay on the ground. Sarah and Andrew would have cheered if their gags had let them.

At that moment the sun broke above the horizon and in the searing beam of its morning glory the princess seemed basked in a halo of gold. The wolves, the pirates and the Urgils drew back in dread, leaving Gublak almost alone before her. Only Ulris dared to stand firm. Peter remained on the ground to his side.

Oswain had seen and heard all from where he lay hidden and now he arose rejoicing. His strong voice resounded from the hill. 'Hail, my sister Alena!' He waved.

Princess Alena turned towards him with a dazzling smile. 'Hail, my brother Oswain!' she cried in response and waved back. At that, the power of Elmesh was released and a beam of silver fire flared from hand to hand between Oswain and his radiant sister. The air crackled with life and everyone's hair stood on end. Awesome in their united strength, the two turned to face Gublak.

Chapter Twenty

FIGHT TO THE FINISH

Everything seemed to happen at once. The beam of light joining Oswain and Princess Alena vanished and suddenly they found themselves grasping a glittering sword each. Oswain reacted immediately. With a triumphant shout he held the weapon aloft and led the forest-folk in a wild charge down the hillside.

Gublak took one look at the assault. 'Attack them!' he screamed. 'Don't let them get the princess. I want her taken alive.'

He rushed forward to seize her. But Peter lashed out with his feet from where he lay. The goblin stumbled and cursed.

'Ulris, kill him,' he commanded angrily.

The leader of the wolf pack needed no second bidding. He bounded forward to where Peter lay on the ground. His wild yellow eyes blazed and his terrible fangs glinted in the sun as he pounced for the kill.

'Look out, Peter,' Princess Alena cried.

With a desperate twist of his body Peter threw himself to one side. The wolf's claws missed by millimetres and Peter felt the brush of fur against his face.

Princess Alena leapt forward and faced the snarling wolf as Peter scrambled to his feet. Ulris' hackles rose, his eyes grew slant and every muscle tensed within his lean frame. The princess flicked a glance at the gleaming sword. It tingled in her grasp. Her heart thumped wildly. She knew one of them would have to die.

They circled one another warily, both looking for the moment to attack. The wolf seemed to grow larger and more powerful in Princess Alena's eyes. Some terrible spirit glowered from within and for a second her heart quailed. He seized his opportunity and, with a soul-destroying howl, hurled himself at the princess's throat.

'No,' screeched Gublak. 'I must have her alive.'

But he was too late. The wolf had leapt to kill.

A huge shadow seemed to envelop the princess as she felt the full supernatural force of the wild wolf-spirit. She fell backwards and the blackness blotted out all hope as it descended upon her. In one final, desperate gesture she thrust upwards with her sword. Then that blade, forged by Elmesh himself, burned with a fiery light and pierced the shadow of death. It plunged into the very heart of the dread wolf. Ulris gave one last howl, twisted away and fell, to rise no more.

Princess Alena lay panting on the ground. She looked at the sword then at the dead wolf. A tremor ran through her body as she thought of what might have happened. She wanted to cry.

But there was no time for that. Peter was by her side helping her to her feet. Oswain and his troops were upon their foes and already a fierce battle was raging all around them. At once the princess found herself in conflict with an Urgil, but his blade was no match for hers and he fell, mortally wounded. Peter seized the dropped sword and began to fight along-side her. Together, they tried to hew their way through the enemy to where they could see Oswain's weapon flashing in the sun.

Fumble had not been idle, meanwhile; he had released both Sarah and Andrew. But being unarmed the three of them stood in great danger.

'Peter! Alena! Help!' cried Sarah above the din of battle.

They turned at the sound of her voice and immediately began to fight their way across to their companion's defence.

The heat of the battle rose; swords crashed and the cries of the warriors filled the air. Wolves hurled themselves into the fray, intent on avenging their leader's death. Urgils thrashed their reptilian tails in deadly sweeps. Their combined forces outnumbered the brave forest-folk almost two to one but, urged on by Oswain, the woodland creatures stoutly held their own.

Stiggle wove in and out among the foe. His sword thrusts were deadly and many an Urgil regretted having confronted this fearless weasel.

A cry for help caught his attention. Grumble was in trouble. Somehow he had fallen and three Urgils surrounded him, intent on his death. Stiggle leapt to his comrade's aid. His sword sliced through the air and one of the Urgils fell.

'That evens up the score a bit,' he cried. 'Come on, Grumble. On your feet.'

The mouse leapt up and together they engaged the two remaining Urgils. It didn't take long to defeat them.

'Thanks,' puffed Grumble. 'I thought I was done for just then.'

'All in a day's work,' Stiggle laughed. 'Hey, there's

Oswain. Look at that sword. Did you ever see anything like it?'

They watched for a moment. Oswain's gleaming blade seemed scarcely to touch his adversaries before they fell. It looked as if nothing could stop him.

'There's a wolf after Fleetfoot,' exclaimed Grumble. 'We'd better help. He's only got a club.'

And with that they dashed to his assistance.

Gublak stood heavily defended by his guards, from where he continually shrieked orders to his troops. He suddenly noticed that up to now the pirates had held back from the fighting.

'Come, you cowards,' cried the goblin. 'A thousand pieces of gold to whoever kills that man.' He pointed to the figure of Oswain. 'And two thousand gold pieces to whoever takes the princess alive.'

That did it. 'Come on, me hearties,' cried Captain Gaspar. 'Let's kill these landlubbers. Slit their throats!'

The band of brigands drew their knives and advanced menacingly into the fray.

But hardly had they started fighting when something happened which changed their minds completely. An awesome, blood-curdling screech rent the air and they saw the mighty Arca sweep into the conflict. Huge white wings thrashed as Elmesh's servant created havoc among his enemies. His eye was on the wolves and his fierce talons plunged into one after another, bringing instant death.

The band of pirates halted in their tracks and dismay filled their hearts as they saw this terrifying addition to the enemy.

'Come on, lads, let's get out of 'ere,' shouted one of the pirates. 'Never mind the gold. I want to keep me 'ead!'

'Hold yer ground,' Captain Gaspar commanded.

But they had seen enough. The pirates turned and fled for their lives.

'Come back, you fools,' screamed Gublak, but even he could not match the terror of the great eagle.

Captain Gaspar hesitated a moment but realized all was lost. He joined his fleeing crew.

Nobody ever knew what happened to those cutthroats. Rumour has it that their flight took them into the marshlands and it may be that the Earth-Trog, denied all else, claimed them as victims. Whatever the truth, they were never seen again.

The battle was turning in favour of Oswain and his companions. Those Urgils and wolves not already dead were weakening under the onslaught. Soon even the ones about Gublak had had enough and, in spite of his threats, fled the battlefield.

And then, it was all over.

Stiggle found himself next to Peter. 'Just like old times,' he laughed.

Peter grinned and wiped the sweat from his brow.

'You were fantastic,' enthused Andrew as he and his sister joined them.

'I really thought Ulris had got you,' said Sarah. She put her arms around her brother's waist. 'I'm glad he didn't.'

Peter smiled. 'So am I,' he said with feeling, and looked towards Princess Alena. 'Still, it's over now. They're all dead.'

'Except for Gublak,' said Andrew. 'Look. Oswain and Alena have got him.'

The four of them made their way among the slain to where Oswain and the princess stood with their captive. The goblin was sullen.

'Well done,' said Oswain. 'All of you. You have shown great courage.'

'Yes, thank you for everything,' said Princess

Alena. 'Without your help all would have been lost. I really am so grateful to you.'

The children felt a bit sheepish all of a sudden.

'It was nothing really,' Peter muttered.

'Nonsense,' Oswain declared. 'Once more you have come to our aid. Elmesh be praised for sending you.'

'Hear, hear,' piped a small voice.

'Hallo, Fumble,' said Oswain. 'You too have done well. You were very brave to go into the enemy camp like that. I am proud of you, my friend.'

The mouse mumbled something in reply. The others laughed.

'Hey, you're sounding like Mumble,' teased Andrew.

'What's that?' said a voice, and Mumble along with Grumble joined the victorious group.

'Are many of our folk wounded?' Oswain enquired of Stiggle.

The weasel looked around. 'Very few I think, sir. But I'll go and check.'

They turned their attention to the defeated goblin.

'Your greed has caused much evil,' Oswain said steadily. 'And to what end? The Star-Pearl would have done you no good and, in any case, it was destined never to be yours. You were doomed to fail and fail you have.'

This was too much for the defeated goblin. He began to gasp and a rattling sound emerged from his throat. His bony hands clenched and unclenched spasmodically. A final madness seemed to come over him and his eyes bulged wildly. He stared at Princess Alena. The Star-Pearl radiated its blue fire, more beautiful than ever before. It seemed to hypnotize the crazed goblin.

'No, it's not true. I have come too far. I must have

it,' he screamed. 'Give it to me. Give it to me!'

Before anyone could stop him he stumbled towards the princess and with one last desperate cry flung himself upon her. She gasped as his greedy fingers closed about the jewel. With a savage wrench he tore the Star-Pearl from her neck and staggered away clutching his glowing prize.

'It's all mine,' he gloated. 'The Star-Pearl is all mine at last!'

Everyone present was stunned by his sudden action. Princess Alena could only stare horror-struck after him. She clutched at her throat and a terrible feeling of foreboding came over her. Oswain at once made to go for the goblin but the evil creature turned on him.

'Do not touch me,' he snarled. 'You were mistaken. You and your friends. Nobody can stop me. . . . Aaghh!'

Gublak screamed. His face contorted and his body writhed in agony. White smoke was pouring from between his fingers. Desperately, he tried to fling the Star-Pearl from him. But he found he couldn't. It seemed stuck to his hands.

The smoke gave way to a dazzling blue light which blinded the eyes of the onlookers. They heard a last long wail of despair from the goblin, then a dull thud. The light faded and there on the ground lay Gublak, the Star-Pearl by his side. He was dead.

Before anyone could move, a mournful howl sounded from the north. Everyone spun round to see what it was. To their dismay, they saw racing across the waste plains the grey twisted funnel of a whirlwind. And they were right in its path. Cold, hard evil filled the rushing air.

'Surin's work!' muttered Oswain. 'He's coming for Alena.'

He strode forward to where the Star-Pearl lay and touched the broken chain with the tip of his sword. There was a hiss and a bright spark. In an instant the chain was restored. But he did not pick it up. Instead, Oswain turned to face his sister.

Princess Alena seemed to be in a trance. She stared wide-eyed at the fast-approaching whirlwind. A hypnotic chanting filled the air, 'Surin . . . Astar . . . Surin . . . Astar . . .'

'Alena!' shouted Sarah. 'Pick up the Star-Pearl. Quickly!'

She gave her a hefty shove which sent her staggering towards Oswain. The princess gazed upon the dead goblin and the jewel. Everyone waited with bated breath. What would she do? The evil whirlwind was almost upon her.

For an agonizing moment she hesitated, then suddenly she stooped to pick up the Star-Pearl. To everyone's relief she replaced it about her neck, and smiled.

The wind died almost instantly and with it the eerie chant. Only a small funnel of debris reached them. But instead of going for the princess it hovered over the dead goblin. They watched in awe as green smoke poured upwards from his body.

Moments later, the whirlwind sped away northwards. All that remained was an empty black robe.

'Phew, that was close,' gasped Peter.

'You're telling me!' Sarah retorted.

Oswain and the princess looked upon the scene in silence.

'I think I feel safe at last,' she said quietly.

'I think so, too.' He grinned and they both laughed. Everyone else joined in.

'Where's Arca?' Andrew asked at length. 'He's surely not gone without saying goodbye.'

He didn't have to wait long for an answer to the question. The eagle soon came swooping back. He carried something in his talons which he dropped at Oswain's feet.

'Ah,' he said. 'Alena, come and see this.'

The princess turned to look.

'Crow!' she exclaimed.

The bird groaned and looked up at the princess. She eyed him sternly.

'You're a traitor, Crow. You have betrayed me and caused much suffering both to myself and my friends. You evil servant of Surin!'

Arca towered over the hapless bird. He waited to deal the death blow to the treacherous creature. But Princess Alena held up a restraining hand.

'Go to your master, Surin,' she commanded. 'Tell him that Alena lives to serve Elmesh. Tell him Astar is dead.'

Crow nodded meekly.

Princess Alena continued, 'And as for you, you are banished for ever from our kingdom. Should you ever dare return, you will be hunted down without mercy. Now, leave at once!'

The last anyone saw of Crow was a small black dot disappearing into the north. Arca's keen eyes never left him until he passed over the distant mountains.

.　　.　　*　　.　　.

An hour later the children, together with Princess Alena and Oswain, found themselves back at Mr and Mrs Trotter's cottage. The badger was delighted to hear of the successful outcome of matters, as he put it.

'But tell me, Princess, what made you decide to

keep the Star-Pearl after all?' he enquired.

'You know, I'm not really sure myself,' she replied thoughtfully. 'You realize, of course, that the news of who I really am—I mean *was*—came as a great shock. I really didn't know what I would do when I met Gublak.

'I suppose it was when he seemed to turn into Surin,' she continued, 'I knew I couldn't resist my natural father and I was about to obey him. That's where Peter bravely came to my help.' She smiled at him and he fidgeted awkwardly. 'I knew then that I had real friends, people who were loyal and kind, and who would even risk their lives for me.'

'Those are the ways of Elmesh,' Trotter murmured.

Princess Alena nodded.

'I know that now,' she said. 'But there's something else, too. It dawned on me that if I gave in to Surin I would have to become like him. The Ice Maiden warned me I would become evil if I lost the Star-Pearl. Suddenly, I saw what that really meant. I would have to kill Peter and Sarah and Andrew to show that I was truly following my father,' she explained. 'And that would have been only the beginning.'

'Phew! I'm glad you didn't do that,' gasped Andrew with relief.

'So am I,' she replied with a wan smile.

'And then what about Gublak?' Sarah added. 'Wasn't that horrendous?'

'He was destroyed by his own greed,' said Oswain. 'But he very nearly gave Surin his chance. I don't think any of us expected that whirlwind. You did well, Sarah.'

She smiled.

'I felt so exposed, so . . .' began Princess Alena.

'Well, that's all in the past,' Trotter interrupted gently. 'Now, what's next?' He glanced in Oswain's direction.

'I think we must get Alena back to Elmar as soon as possible,' he answered. 'Our parents will be very concerned and we should not delay. I will ask Arca to go on ahead and give them the good news.'

He rose to his feet.

'Can we come, too?' Peter asked. 'We've never been to Elmar.'

Oswain smiled. 'But of course. Indeed, it is high time I paid a visit myself. We shall journey together.'

.　　.　　*　　.　　.

The three children were a little sad that their stay in the Great Forest could not be longer, but they managed to get round to most of their old friends throughout the rest of that day. All the talk was about the battle, naturally enough, and the older ones spent much time comparing it with the time when they had fought Hagbane. And, as is usual, the tales grew in the telling until almost everyone was a hero. Remarkably, nobody had been killed, but those who had been wounded were paraded around as the greatest heroes of all.

Early next morning, after many fond farewells, the party set off happily on their journey to Elmar. It took them three days, which was quicker than it might otherwise have been, because Oswain found some friendly horses who would allow them to ride upon their backs.

Arca had fulfilled his mission and upon reaching the gates of the city they were delighted to find the whole place in a festive mood. Banners decorated the walls and hundreds of flag-waving people lined the streets and cheered the small procession as it wended its way towards the palace. The three children marvelled at their reception.

'Cor, this is all right, isn't it?' said Andrew. 'It's like being royalty.'

'Well we are, silly,' his sister laughed. 'At least Oswain and Alena are. Don't they look splendid?'

It was not long before the company reached the palace gates, where they were saluted by the guards. All at once they were out of the crowds and approaching the drive towards the main entrance of the palace itself.

And there stood the aged King and Queen. Princess Alena slipped from her horseback and ran to meet her parents. She flung her arms about them.

'We thought you were lost, child,' sobbed the Queen. 'Elmesh be praised, you have returned.'

'And you have made the right choice,' smiled her father. 'That is even better news to my ears.'

'Yes, Father,' the princess smiled through glistening eyes.

The old King turned towards his son. 'Well, Oswain, are you going to sit there all day? Come down and greet your parents.'

Oswain laughed and dismounted. He went forward and grasped his father's hands warmly. He kissed his mother.

'Now, you must introduce your companions,' said the King. 'We have heard much about them.'

The three children were brought before him and they bowed low.

'Tch, enough of that,' he said. 'I grow too old for all this ceremony. Just treat me like an uncle, will you?'

The children laughed and immediately felt at ease

with the amiable old King. He put his arms around Sarah and Andrew and together they climbed the steps of the magnificent palace. The rest of the party followed.

The King stopped at the door and turned to the others with a twinkle in his eye.

'Now come along, Alena. You go first,' he said. 'We have a little surprise for you.'

As Princess Alena entered the palace she gasped with amazement. The great hall was jam-packed with all the nobles, officials and servants of the palace, and straight before her was a simply enormous birthday cake. At a signal from the King the palace orchestra struck up and everyone began to sing.

The princess was quite overcome when they applauded her and didn't know what to say.

'This is to make up for the party you missed,' the King chuckled. 'Come now, everybody, let us have a really good feast. Alena has come of age and is back with us. Oswain is here, too. I am a very happy father indeed.'

Nobody needed a second bidding and soon the great hall was resounding to the noise of cheerful conversation and the clattering of cutlery as everyone tucked in.

'Wow, am I glad we came!' Andrew garbled through a mouthful of cake.

Chapter Twenty-one

RESCUED!

Princess Alena's birthday party was a great success. She herself looked quite radiant and wore the Star-Pearl proudly as she mingled with the guests. Everyone fussed over Peter, Sarah and Andrew, especially as rumours of their exploits spread around the hall. Much to Andrew's delight there was a simply enormous amount of food and he gorged himself to his heart's content.

Oswain spent much of the time deep in conversation with his parents and the Lord Chancellor. Clearly, the full story of Princess Alena's past had serious implications for the Kingdom of the West.

'I bet Oswain's telling them everything about Alena and Surin,' said Andrew through yet another cream bun. He choked on a crumb.

'That'll teach you to talk with your mouth full,' his sister laughed. 'And you'll be sick in a minute if you eat much more!'

Peter interrupted before Andrew could think of a suitable reply. 'I wonder what they'll do? Do you think they can really trust Alena now?'

'Surin might declare war, anyway,' Sarah added.

Their ponderings were cut short by the Lord Chancellor who clapped his hands and called silence for the King.

'My lords, ladies and gentlemen,' the King began. 'Thank you all for coming to celebrate our daughter's fifteenth birthday, even though for some reason which, ahem, has slipped my mind, it is a little late.'

A ripple of laughter went around the hall.

The King continued: 'A strange tale has been told me by Oswain, the details of which I will not bore you with now. Nevertheless, many adventures have befallen our princess and great destinies have been decided as a result.'

He paused for breath.

'As you see, I and the Queen grow old and it will not be many years before Elmesh calls us. Another must then rule the City of Elmar and the Wester lands. I am proud to say there is one who has proved worthy of that honour and I would like now to name my successor.'

A small ripple ran across the room. The King waited for silence.

'By the will of Elmesh, I declare my daughter, Princess Alena, to be the lawful heir to the throne upon my departure,' he announced with a smile.

All present applauded. The princess looked somewhat abashed but pleased.

'Furthermore,' the King added, 'a highway shall be built between the City of Elmar and the Great Forest. Resting houses will be set up along the way. As you appreciate, Alena is of tender years and there will be need of talk between her and Oswain. Who can tell what the future may hold? Yet this I know. Two swords have been wondrously forged from one fiery bond. Thus, a brother and sister shall between them hold the great lands of the East and West in the harmony of Elmesh's will.'

There were many cries of 'Hear, hear' to this.

Oswain and Princess Alena smiled at one another. Both carried their blades sheathed at their sides.

'One other matter remains,' said the King. 'I have been told of the exploits of Peter, Sarah and Andrew. Without their loyalty and courage, matters would have taken a very different course and I would have been a grieving father this day.

'These must soon return to their own realm. But I would wish them to depart with our gratitude and, should they ever come back, to be held in highest honour.' He turned to the children.

'Would you come forward, please.'

They did as they were bidden and stood before him. All of a sudden, they felt ashamed of their grubby clothes.

The King sensed their embarrassment and addressed them. 'In our kingdom poor clothing is no mark of shame, especially when such garments speak of honourable deeds. Kneel before me.' He whispered, 'Have to do these things properly, you know.'

The King took a great sword from the Lord Chancellor and with it dubbed the three children in turn.

'Arise, Sir Peter,' he cried. 'Arise, Lady Sarah. Arise, Sir Andrew. I pronounce you free knights of the realm.'

There was more applause and much cheering.

'Well, well, that is all,' said the King. 'Carry on eating, everyone.'

'Coo, it doesn't half make you feel good, doesn't it?' Andrew exclaimed. 'Fancy being knighted!' Peter and Sarah smiled to each other.

Oswain came across and offered them his congratulations. From then on the children had a steady stream of people doing the same. They felt quite overwhelmed.

At last, they were joined by Princess Alena and her

mother.

'Thank you,' the princess said simply.

The Queen looked upon Peter, Sarah and Andrew with her serene grey eyes. 'You have fought well against forces whose power is far greater than ever you could imagine,' she said in a soft voice. 'Our kingdom has been saved and our daughter restored. I do thank you.'

The King and Oswain approached. 'Well, well. What a happy day,' chortled the jovial old man. 'Now, are you staying long? The palace is yours for as long as you wish, and the freedom of the City, of course.'

'Well, actually, we'd love to stay, your Highness,' Peter began.

'But they need to return to their own realm, Father,' Oswain finished for him.

The boy nodded.

'Oh, deary me. Yes, of course. Well, how are we going to do that?'

'The Tower of Visions,' the Queen said quietly.

'Then so shall it be. We will go there at once.'

Somehow the children knew this was the right moment to depart, so they accompanied the royal family up a staircase which led into a lofty tower. They entered an empty room with seven windows set in seven walls.

'It will not be possible to return you to exactly where you came from,' Oswain explained. 'To do that would mean going down to the sea, which would take too long. But we will trust Elmesh to see you through safely.'

'Well, goodbye,' said the King. He shook hands with the boys and kissed Sarah.

Oswain and the Queen did likewise.

'It feels so sad to be going,' said Sarah. 'It would be

wonderful if we could stay for ever.'

Princess Alena stepped forward. 'I hope we meet again sometime,' she said. 'You really have become good friends to me. I shall miss you.'

With that she said goodbye to Sarah and Andrew. But she kissed Peter. 'That's for being a special friend,' she grinned. He blushed slightly and heard Andrew chuckle behind him.

Oswain took charge of the proceedings. He indicated a lamp which hung above their heads.

'Concentrate upon the light,' he said, 'and do not be afraid. Farewell, my friends.'

The children obeyed and the room flooded with blue light. A rushing noise filled their ears. They felt themselves floating upwards and seemed far away from anywhere. The sound turned into a gentle swishing and each felt they were drifting in a dream.

Peter wondered why his feet felt cold. Surely the duvet had not fallen off his bed. He could still hear the rushing noise all around him. Suddenly, he came to his senses. He was not in bed, as he thought, but standing on a rock in the midst of the sea. The cold was water splashing over his feet and the sound was that of the waves. Sarah and Andrew were both with him.

'Ugh,' cried Sarah. 'It's cold.'

'And wet,' Andrew added. 'Where are we?'

'I'll tell you,' Peter said grimly as he gathered his wits together. 'We're stuck on a rock and we're cut off by the tide. Look!'

They followed his gaze. All around them the sea hissed and splashed. Ahead was the cliff face and they could make out the entrance to the tunnel of the round hole. But there was no way they could reach it.

'Can't we swim for it?' Andrew suggested.

'Not a chance,' his brother replied. 'We'd be

smashed to pieces against these rocks.'

'Then what are we going to do?' Sarah shrieked.

'I don't know,' Peter replied.

'Look, there's someone on the cliff up there.' Andrew pointed out some small figures. 'Start shouting and waving.'

'Huh, they're only little kids,' said Peter after a few moments. 'They're waving back. They think it's a game.'

Just then another figure appeared. It looked like a man. He took one look, waved to them, then ran off.

'Phew. I think he's realized we're in trouble,' said Peter. 'He's gone for help.' Then he added as an afterthought, 'At least, I hope he has.'

'Well, he'd better be quick,' Andrew said. 'The tide's coming in all the time.'

All three scrambled to the top of the rock and waited. The waves and the spray soaked them right through and they felt very cold. Sarah noticed they were back in their light summer clothes.

'How long've we got, d'you reckon?' Andrew asked.

'Dunno,' Peter replied. 'Ten minutes or so. I've no idea really.'

'Mum and Dad will kill us when they find out,' Sarah groaned. 'What'll we say?'

'Tell them the truth, I guess. We always do. But they'll never believe us, of course,' her younger brother replied.

Just then they heard a new sound above the roar of the sea. A steady thrumming came from round the headland. It grew louder.

'Hey! Look,' cried Andrew. 'It's a helicopter. Wave your hands.'

The bright yellow shape of an RAF Sea King whirled into view. The noise grew deafening as it banked and hovered above the cliff.

'They've seen us,' cried Sarah. 'Hurray!'

A voice barked from a loudhailer. 'Stay calm. There's no need to panic. I'm sending a man down to lift you off one by one.'

The helicopter hovered overhead and they could feel the powerful downdraft from its massive five-bladed rotor. Even the waves flattened out under its force. The whine from the twin turboshafts made it almost impossible to hear anything else.

Moments later a figure appeared to step into space from the right-hand side of the machine and they watched open-mouthed as he winched down towards them. After a few trial swings he landed on the rock.

'Everyone all right?' he shouted. 'No broken bones or anything?'

'No, we're fine,' Peter yelled back.

'Okay, missy,' he smiled at Sarah. 'Ladies first, I reckon. Stick your arms through here and I'll come up with you. Won't be long, lads.'

Sarah obeyed and was soon snug in the special rescue harness. The crewman waved and, in an instant, Sarah was whisked off the rock. It was a scary feeling and the hawser looked very thin. She was glad the man was with her and she clutched him tightly.

The view was dizzying. She glanced down. Peter and Andrew looked like little white ants on their tiny rock and she marvelled at the skill of the helicopter crew. In a few moments, they were level with the hatch and another crewman helped them into the cabin and on to the deck.

'Mind the edge now,' he said to Sarah. 'You're safe.' He helped her out of the sling. 'All right, George?'

'Okay, Bill,' said the crewman. Seconds later and

he was gone again.

It took only about five minutes to have all three children winched to safety but by now quite a crowd had gathered on the cliff top. The pilot manoeuvred until his helicopter was over the grassy top.

'Stand clear. Everyone stand well back,' he barked through the loudhailer. 'I'm coming in to land. Everyone stand well clear.'

It took some minutes before he felt it safe enough to bring the great machine down. The boys especially would have loved to look all over the helicopter but as soon as they touched down and the engines reduced to tick-over, George ordered all three out.

Just as they were walking clear a man and a woman broke from the crowd and came dashing towards them.

'It's Mum and Dad,' cried Sarah.

She ran into her mother's arms.

'Oh, I'm so glad you're safe,' sobbed Mrs Brown. 'We didn't know where you had got to these last two hours.'

The boys were joined by their father. He looked grim.

'What happened, Peter?' he demanded. 'Where have you all been?'

'Sorry, Dad. We were cut off by the tide . . .'

'Of all the stupid . . .'

He was cut short by the crewman, George.

'Are you their father, sir?'

He nodded. 'I'm terribly sorry about all this. I've always taught them to be careful of the tides. I just don't know what got into them.'

'Well, it happens all the time,' George smiled. 'Good job we were in the area. Not everyone's so lucky. Anyway they're safe and sound now and that's what matters. Don't be too hard on them, sir.'

Mr Brown was a good father. He smiled back. 'No, I won't,' he said.

While he and the crewman sorted out the details for a report, the children stood with their mother.

'I wish everyone wouldn't keep staring at us,' Andrew muttered.

'It's because you're celebrities,' his mother replied. 'After all, it's not every day you see a real live air–sea rescue. They'll soon go, don't worry. Now, tell me what happened.'

You're not going to believe this, Mum. . . .' Peter began.

.   .   *   .   .

The next morning, Peter, Sarah and Andrew were again walking on the cliff top. They wanted to have another look at where they had been rescued, though their father had given them very strict instructions not to descend the round hole or go on the rocks.

'I knew they wouldn't believe us,' said Andrew.

'Never mind,' his brother grinned. '*We* know what happened.'

'I still wish we hadn't given Mum and Dad such a fright,' said Sarah. 'They thought we'd been daydreaming.'

'Wasn't it good in the helicopter?' said Andrew. 'I wouldn't mind doing that again.'

'Once is enough for me,' said Sarah primly.

'I wonder what will happen to Alena now?' Peter murmured.

'I'd like to know what Surin will do,' Andrew said. 'I bet he was furious with Crow.'

'He was a nasty bit of work, that bird,' said Peter.

They reached the round hole and lay on their stomachs to peer over the rim.

'Hey, what's that down there?' Andrew asked.

They followed his finger. There, lying quite dead at the bottom of the hole, was a large black bird.

It was a crow.

Hagbane's Doom
A tale of heroism, adventure, and the age-old conflict between good and evil

by John Houghton

Introducing...

Peter, Sarah and Andrew—three ordinary children caught up in an adventure that proves to be far from ordinary.

Trotter, Aldred, Stiggle and company—a band of lovable animals united in the fight against a wicked tyrant.

Hagbane—an evil witch who rules the Great Forest with a bitter hatred and an iron will.

Oswain—a prince whose destiny not even he will fully understand until he looks into the enchanted pool.

Children of all ages (and there's no upper limit!) will enjoy this gripping fantasy which portrays the power of love and goodness in the face of evil.

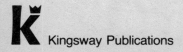

Kingsway Publications

Surin's Revenge

by John Houghton

Trouble is brewing in the North. Surin's army is preparing for war. An evil sorcerer has offered him his long-awaited chance to take vengeance on the South.

If he succeeds, Oswain and his kingdom will be destroyed. Oswain's only hope is to find the Ice Maiden before it is too late.

Peter and Sarah join him in a dramatic race against time. Meanwhile, Andrew and his scruffy dog Tatters seek help from a band of fugitive slaves.

But will this tiny company be any match for the might of Surin's army? What will become of all their friends if his terrifying plans succeed?

This is the third story in The Oswain Tales, following on from *Hagbane's Doom* and *Gublak's Greed*.

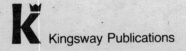

Kingsway Publications

The Pilgrim's Progress
Retold in today's English

by James H. Thomas

Christian's Journey

Bunyan's famous allegory has a permanent place among English classics. But far more important, it has been a source of spiritual inspiration and help to countless readers since it was first published three hundred years ago.

The Pilgrim's Progress is a book that every Christian should read, but today many find its archaic language hard to follow. In this version the story is retold in a style that today's readers can understand and enjoy, while losing none of the original spiritual thrust and challenge.

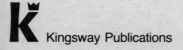

Kingsway Publications